Play the Bach, Dear!

Play the Bach, Dear!

Judith Groch

Doubleday & Company, Inc.
Garden City, New York

Library of Congress Catalog Card Number 77–76960
ISBN: 0-385-13228-X Trade
ISBN: 0-385-13229-8 Library

To Deborah, Emily, and Peter

CONTENTS

PLAY THE BACH, DEAR!

1

Prelude

"How dumb can you get!" Waldo stared down at his sister Hilary, who was folded in the Prayer Position on the floor in front of the piano.

K'choo! Hilary lifted her head, flung her long honey-colored hair out of her eyes, and wiped her nose. The thick, woolly nap of the living-room rug got in her nostrils and tickled.

"Waldo Banister," she said, glowering, "if you don't stop kidding around and come here and recite the magic words this minute, I'll put a curse on *you*—for the whole rest of your life. Hurry, before she comes!" With that, Hilary plopped her face back into the rug and waited for her brother to begin.

Nothing happened.

Hilary was eleven years old, tall for her age, and about

to have an exceptionally bad piano lesson. Waldo was eight and three quarters and a pest. He had wavy brown hair, pointy ears, and his mother's big brown eyes—everyone said.

Sticking his tongue into his bubble gum, Waldo blew a big pink bubble and watched it cross-eyed until it went POP. Then he walked around his sister and examined her critically. On her knees, with her head down between her extended arms, and her hair thrown forward over her head, Hilary reminded Waldo of a broken umbrella, turned inside out.

"Your underpants show," he said.

Hilary flung herself back on her heels. "Don't be disgusting, Waldo," she said. "I don't usually go crawling around on my hands and knees praying to the gods for protection."

Then her voice softened. "Waldo, please, it's almost four o'clock. Miss Orpheo's going to ring the doorbell. Say the Piano-lesson Spell—QUICK—or my lesson will be a disaster."

"It'll be anyway," said Waldo sweetly.

"Then a double disaster!"

Waldo was absolutely maddening. It had often occurred to Hilary that she might recite the magic spell herself. Yet, she didn't think it would work. If you were going to use a magic spell, you might as well do it properly. "Properly" meant that someone had to chant the words over you, while you concentrated on letting all its protection seep through your body from your toes to the tips of your fingers. Hilary wasn't certain that the magic words helped; Miss Orpheo could always tell when you hadn't practiced and would yell anyway. On the other hand, to come to her lesson without the magic words would be like sitting down at the piano naked. Although clothing didn't exactly make you play better, Hilary could imagine playing much worse without it.

Tick tock. In the front hall, the large grandfather clock stared straight ahead, dignified and aloof.

Down on the floor, Hilary was getting desperate. "Waldo, please hurry . . . She's almost here. If you don't quit horsing around I'll . . . I'll have an attack!"

"What kind of attack?"

"A heart attack, stupid."

"Mom says children don't get heart attacks."

"Wallll-DO!" Raising herself on one arm, Hilary swung a karate chop in her brother's direction.

Tick tock . . . tick tock.

"I'll let you use my record player," Hilary coaxed.

"Mom said if you'd practice instead of praying . . ."

"Oh shut UP, Mr. Smarty-pants!"

"O.K., O.K.," Waldo grumbled. "Relax!" He stashed the bubble gum in his pocket and set to work. Pressing the palms of his hands together, he lowered his eyes and assumed what he hoped was a very solemn expression. (Waldo did look serious, but he also looked asleep.) Then, stirring the air with great sweeping movements, he intoned the words of the magic spell.

> *"Brahms, Beethoven, Mozart, Gluck,*
> *Hello, Good-bye, Good Hope, Good Luck!"*

"Who's Gluck?" he interrupted.

"Walll-DO! A famous opera composer—and besides,

he rhymes!" Hilary was angry. "Now you'll have to start all over again. The magic doesn't work if you stop in the middle."

The clock in the hall sounded. The rug tickled. Hilary softened. "Please, Waldo, be serious or we'll never get through."

Waldo began again. Hilary clenched her fists, squeezed her eyes shut, and concentrated. A deep feeling of calm and strength spread through her body as the words of the spell enveloped her in their protective magic.

"Brahms, Beethoven, Mozart, Gluck," Waldo recited obediently, "Hello, Good-bye . . ."

Something was wrong. Hilary sensed an ominous rearrangement in the air behind her, as if some of it had shifted to make room for something else to occupy its space. It began to crush down on her, growing warmer and thicker.

Waldo had stopped chanting. The room was silent.

Abruptly, Hilary sat up, swiveled around on her heels, and saw . . . Ohmygod! There, staring down at her, in her brown ragpicker dress and her rummage-sale shoes, stood Miss Orpheo. How long had the teacher been standing there? How much had she heard?

"That is a rather ungraceful position, Hilary," said Miss Orpheo unpleasantly. "Have you lost something?"

Hilary scrambled to her feet and shook the hair out of her mouth. "I was just . . . just hunting for my bus pass," she stammered. Her cheeks were glowing hot. She wanted to crawl under the rug.

"I see. And have you found it?" inquired Miss Orpheo, leaning toward Hilary.

"Yes. I mean, no." Out of the corner of her eye she could see Waldo inching backward out of the room. But the doorbell hadn't rung. "Did I leave the door open?"

"Fortunately, no," replied Miss Orpheo in a tight, birdy voice. She enunciated each syllable as if it might fly away. "One can't be too careful these days," she observed. "Especially in an apartment house."

For a moment Hilary's eyes blurred. She blinked. Miss Orpheo looked out of focus. Faded at the edges. If the door was closed, how had Miss Orpheo . . .

"As long as we take precautions," continued Miss Orpheo, interrupting Hilary's thoughts, "nothing untoward is likely to happen."

Miss Orpheo worried about Untoward Things, instead of plain ordinary robbers and muggers. Raised at a time when people still had Values and Character, Miss Orpheo insisted that her pupils wear their hair tied back out of their eyes and that they avoid extremes of dress. Her own hair framed her long face like window curtains and then wound tightly around her head in a coronet of braids. Miss Orpheo abhorred pants, short skirts, tight anything, and jewelry. "Away from the piano," she was fond of saying, "you may dress as you please. But in the presence of this glorious instrument, let us show our respect by appearing in suitable attire." Miss Orpheo was in love with pianos. She probably liked them better than people. Still, Hilary wondered, how did she get in?

Miss Orpheo moved across the room. Reaching into the depths of her hideous crocheted pocketbook, she extracted a pencil and her eyeglasses. "If you are quite certain, Hilary, that your bus pass does not repose on the floor, perhaps we may turn our attention to music." She waved Hilary to the piano.

While Hilary opened her music to the right page, Miss Orpheo checked to see that the metronome was wound. It was. Nobody ever used it. Carefully, Miss Orpheo smoothed her skirt and settled herself in the chair at Hilary's right. Hilary could feel the teacher's eyes drilling through her.

Miss Orpheo opened Hilary's notebook.

> Sept. 29. Lift fingers in Bach. Hands quiet.
> Mazurka—play hands separately. *Count!*
> THINK!

"Shall we take your scales first?" Miss Orpheo asked —as if there were a choice!

Miss Orpheo adored scales. "Each scale," she was fond of saying, "is a friend." According to Miss Orpheo, the scales had different personalities: C-sharp major, with seven sharps, was haughty and sophisticated; humble C major, the friend of children; D major, bright and spirited. How could anyone get so worked up about a bunch of corroded scales! But that was Miss Orpheo. Music did things to her.

"Begin with A-flat major," Miss Orpheo directed.

Hilary drew a deep breath and wiped her sweaty hands on the side of her skirt.

"Remember now, loose wrists, Play in*n*to the keys. Fingers high . . . little soldiers marching up the scale."

Carried away by the A-flat major scale (a sunny, out-door scale to Miss Orpheo; a finger-trap to Hilary), Miss Orpheo was working her long, bony fingers up and down in the air, playing an imaginary piano.

Hilary made a face and began. A-flat, B-flat . . . She put the wrong finger on C, and within four notes had run out of fingers. She began again. The right fingering this time—but she forgot the D-flat. She began again, stumbled, and suddenly she couldn't remember what scale she was playing.

Miss Orpheo frowned and clapped her hands impa-tiently. "Hilary! Did you practice your scales?"

"Umm," Hilary mumbled. "Not enough, I guess." Well, it was true, she *had* practiced them—yesterday.

"In that case," said Miss Orpheo, "please be good enough to learn them for next week." When Miss Or-pheo was angry, her chin puckered into a tight little cir-cle, her long nose extended, and her voice seemed to come out of her ears. If there was one thing Miss Orpheo detested, it was to hear the same mistakes two weeks in a row, three weeks in a row . . . Hilary gulped.

"Do your finger exercises." Clasping her hands in her lap, Miss Orpheo rearranged the features of her face in a friendlier, more hopeful expression.

The stupid finger exercises were even worse.

Miss Orpheo sighed. "Hilary," she inquired wearily, "how long do you practice each day?"

"About three quarters of an hour," said Hilary softly, stretching it as much as she dared.

Miss Orpheo scowled. "I expect you to practice at least an hour every day."

Every day! Hilary rolled her eyes. If Miss Orpheo only knew. Hilary never practiced on the day after her lesson. After all, she told herself, a person deserved a little reward for having survived the ordeal. Also, Hilary rarely practiced on the weekend, because . . . well, because it was the weekend.

"What else do you have?" Miss Orpheo asked. The piano teacher knew perfectly well what else Hilary had. She was probably checking on whether *Hilary* knew what else she had.

"The Czerny exercise," she answered unhappily.

"Very good," said Miss Orpheo. "I want to hear each note clearly and distinctly." Miss Orpheo leaned forward, waiting to hear the bright, crisp notes.

There were none. Poor Miss Orpheo. At one point Hilary's right hand hurried ahead of Hilary's left hand. It sounded awful.

Hilary turned crimson. Miss Orpheo turned pale. A strange expression passed over the teacher's face, as if something inside were caving in. Immediately, the features came together again, sharp and focused. Yet there was something wrong with Miss Orpheo. Hilary glanced at her teacher and for a fleeting moment she had the peculiar sensation that Miss Orpheo wasn't there. Hilary blinked her eyes, shook her head, and the feeling was gone.

Then she looked down and noticed. She had forgotten to cut her fingernails. Miss Orpheo was a bug on having nails short. Oh God! It was too late now to cut her nails —or for that matter, she decided, her throat!

2

THE LESSON

The magic spell wasn't helping, Hilary thought gloomily as she went crashing through her Bach Invention. Deep in her heart, of course, she knew that magic spells worked better if you practiced during the week. Playing the Bach was like riding a roller-coaster. One wrong note and whoooeeeee . . . You were off, hurtling into outer space.

"No! No!" cried Miss Orpheo, rapping her pencil on the arm of her chair. "When you have mastered all that Bach has to teach you, then you may begin to compose your own music. Until then, Hilary, I suggest you play the music as Bach wrote it."

After massacring the Bach, Hilary turned with relief to her Chopin Mazurka. She liked the Mazurka; she had even practiced it. But by now her fingers were having a nervous breakdown. The beginning of the Mazurka, with its long, curving melody, went well enough. Miss Orpheo let her continue. Hilary relaxed and took a deep breath. Then the music changed and again she was in trouble. Hilary hated this part. Anyone with an ounce of sense could see it ruined the Mazurka. Chopin had probably written it one day when he was in a ratty mood—just to make her life miserable.

"A mazurka is a dance," scolded Miss Orpheo, waggling her fingers through the air. "You must make it sound so." Rising from her seat, she reached around Hilary with one arm, and over Hilary's shoulder with the other. Her pointed chin grazed Hilary's head as she demonstrated the passage. Locked in the magic circle of her teacher's arms, Hilary sat and held her breath. Miss Orpheo smelled of lemon.

Why was it, Hilary wondered, that whenever Miss Orpheo played a new piece for her, it always sounded so promising. Each time, Hilary would hope that finally Hilary Banister would play something so fantastic that people would stop to exclaim, "How beautiful! Who's playing?" But by the time Hilary had finished taming the music, the magic would be gone. Instead of "How beautiful!" people said, "Oh, *must* you?" And if they didn't say it, they thought it. Why was it necessary to destroy something in order to learn it? Hilary wondered. If she studied piano long enough, she realized, she might succeed in destroying all the music that had ever been written. Hmm!

"Hilary! You are not concentrating," exclaimed Miss Orpheo.

"Should I do the 'Träumerei' next?"

"By all means."

Schumann's dreamy little piece had received its kiss of death three weeks earlier. Yuch! Hilary began to play. Blah blaaah . . . blah, blah, blah, blah . . .

"No Hilary, NO!" cried Miss Orpheo. "You must count!" And seizing the metronome, she adjusted its speed and set the horrible thing ticking.

Tick-tick, went the metronome. Blah blaaah went the Träumerei. It was impossible to play with that idiot machine ticking its head off. Suddenly, Hilary's fingers tangled and tripped.

Up jumped Miss Orpheo. Down fell the crocheted pocketbook. "No NO!" she cried. "You are all tense and tight!" Ducking her head to the floor, she retrieved her pocketbook, slung it over the arm of her chair, and just as abruptly, dropped back into her seat as if she had come unwound.

"Look how you hold your hands: stiff, all stiff!" And to demonstrate, Miss Orpheo stuck her long finger into the back of Hilary's hand, poking away at all the tense, knotted-up spots only Miss Orpheo knew were there.

"And the wrists . . . like wood!" Grasping Hilary's right arm, Miss Orpheo lifted it in the air and shook it. She let go suddenly. The arm stayed up. "You cannot play like that! Everything must be LOOSE!"

Hilary lowered her arm and sighed. She had never seen Miss Orpheo so worked up. Even the coronet of braids, wound around Miss Orpheo's long head, seemed to have trouble hanging on.

Next, Miss Orpheo tried to show Hilary how to loosen her hand and wrist muscles. Naturally, the more the teacher poked Hilary's hand, flapping it from the wrist, and the more she shouted, "Relax!" the stiffer and tighter everything got. It was difficult to relax with someone yelling RELAX at you and stabbing holes into the back of your hand.

Finally, shaking her head, Miss Orpheo announced, "We need the Loosening-up Exercises! Come. Stand up." And bolting from her chair, Miss Orpheo motioned Hilary toward the center of the room.

Hilary was dangerously close to tears. They'd been doing the stupid Loosening-up Exercises for four years, and Hilary still couldn't see what bending over and swinging her fingers and toes, or chasing around the room wriggling her wrists and flapping her arms had to do with playing the piano. The Loosening-up Exercises were for the birds. Literally, for the *birds*. Hilary knew what was coming.

"Up-Down, Up-Down," sang Miss Orpheo, bending in half from the waist. "ALL the way down . . . to your toes . . . wrists loose . . . hands around in circles."

Gritting her teeth, Hilary hung over her toes, rotating her hands in stiff little squares. It was humiliating.

"Good. GOOD!" Miss Orpheo urged Hilary on. "And now, UP we go, around the room on wings of air, like a bird. A bird must be relaxed to fly, you know."

I didn't ask to fly, Hilary muttered to herself. Besides, birds didn't play the piano.

Damn! Damn!

Around and around the room flew Miss Orpheo,

bending to the floor, then straightening up, her brown ragpicker dress with its loose sleeves fluttering as her long arms flailed the air. At times her feet barely seemed to touch the floor.

Around and around the room went poor, miserable Hilary, waving her arms in a feeble imitation of Miss Orpheo.

"Let yourself go!" cried Miss Orpheo, accelerating her wingbeats. Good thing the window was closed, thought Hilary. The woman was practically flying. The flabby, loose flesh of Miss Orpheo's throat and chin jerked up and down like a shopping bag beneath her angular jaw. One wing up, the other down, Miss Orpheo banked awkwardly for a turn at the corner of the room and almost crash-landed on the piano. Yich. The whole thing was degrading.

Cruising behind Miss Orpheo, Hilary passed the living-room door and caught a glimpse of Waldo and his pal Stevie crouching behind the door, trying to smother their laughter. Stevie's eyes were popping out of his head. Waldo looked as if he were about to swallow his face. He started to giggle. Hilary pinned her brother with a murderous look and flicked a wing at him to indicate a slit throat. Then, waving her arms and flapping her hands, she flew off after Miss Orpheo.

Finally, Miss Orpheo decided that Hilary was sufficiently relaxed. Pausing to catch her breath, the teacher stabbed a hairpin into the lopsided coronet of braids, which had lost its struggle to remain aloft and now sagged down over her ears. She adjusted her dress on her bony shoulders and returned to the piano. The lesson resumed its dreary course.

Hilary smoothed her hair and glanced sideways at Miss Orpheo. She looked tired and defeated. For a moment, Hilary felt sorry for her. She couldn't blame music teachers for preferring pupils with talent, or at least, *some* ability. After all, they had to make a living, and it was certainly better to teach someone for whom there was hope. And *that*, thought Hilary, clamping her teeth shut, let Hilary Banister out! Hadn't Aunt Ottilie said it?

Once, after listening to Hilary play, Aunt Ottilie had remarked to Hilary's mother, "When the good Lord was busy giving out Talent—tch tch—he must have forgotten about You-Know-Who." That had hurt. Aunt Ottilie-Big-Mouth was always making snide remarks like that, right in front of you, because somehow she believed that children were deaf, or if not deaf, then stupid, and if not stupid, then too young to understand when they were being insulted. Hilary never forgave Aunt Ottilie for her fatal words; neither did she forget them. She suspected Aunt Ottilie was right.

"Hilary, please . . . you are not concentrating," scolded Miss Orpheo.

Of course, Hilary thought, it would be nice to be talented—to be able to play as well as Adrian Scorn, who was a musical genius, or Lyra Lyons. Lyra Lyons played anything that could be played: cello, flute, clarinet, you name it—in addition to the piano, which she'd been playing only two years. Lyra Lyons could sing, too. Otherwise, Lyra Lyons was a big fat goody-goody whose only friends were her cello, her flute, her clarinet, her piano, and, Hilary supposed, her music teachers.

It wasn't Hilary's fault that she'd turned out to be the most untalented musical disaster that had ever sat in front of a piano. Mr. Harrison, their science teacher, had taught them about *that*. It had something to do with little things you couldn't see called genes which you inherited from your parents. Like the color of your eyes, talent was arranged before you were born. Bach and his children had it. Mozart had it. Hilary sighed. When Mozart was eight years old, he was composing music Hilary Banister couldn't have played in a million years. Adrian Scorn and Lyra Lyons had it.

"Talent is not enough, Hilary," said Miss Orpheo unexpectedly. "You must work hard. You must have courage and, perhaps," she added, "something else—luck."

Hilary was startled. At times Miss Orpheo almost seemed able to read her mind. She started to ask, "What do you mean by 'luck'?" but as she looked at Miss Orpheo, she had the peculiar feeling she could see right through her. Hilary blinked her eyes and the teacher again appeared solid enough.

In the hall, the clock struck five. At last Miss Orpheo arose and collected her belongings. She dropped her pencil and eyeglasses into her pocketbook and snapped it shut. Then she took her coat, went to the front door, and with a shake of her head, disappeared.

"I could swear she disappeared right in front of me," Hilary said to Waldo later. "Just blinked out."

"Really?" said Waldo. "Let me watch next time she's

here." Hilary couldn't decide whether he meant it seriously.

At five-thirty Mrs. Banister came home from the hospital, where she supervised a painting class in the Rehabilitation Center. She found Hilary sitting on her bed, scissors in hand, trying to do her social studies homework. Magazines and newspaper pages were strewn all over the bed, the desk, and the floor.

"Mom," said Hilary as her mother appeared in the room, "do you know where I can find a picture of air pollution?"

"Try the newspaper, dear," said Mrs. Banister wearily. "It's filled with it these days."

"I did," said Hilary, angrily flipping through the pages of the newspaper. "There's nothing. When you *don't* need them, you can find all the pictures you want. It's really weird."

With a start, Mrs. Banister realized what Hilary was doing. "HILARY! Is that today's paper?"

"Yup. And yesterday's, and the day-before-yesterday's, and . . ."

"Hilary, how many times have I told you not to cut up the newspaper before your father has read it? He hates an untidy paper."

"I haven't cut anything," Hilary explained patiently. "There isn't anything." Why didn't teachers ask you to bring in news when it was still news?

Mrs. Banister was bending over, collecting the scattered pages of the paper, shoving and shaking them all back together again. She found a sock under Hilary's bed and asked what it was doing there.

Finally the paper was restored. "By the way, dear," said Mrs. Banister as she turned to go, "how was your piano lesson?"

"O.K.," said Hilary with a shrug.

"I'm so glad," said her mother, smiling at last. "As I've said all the time, all you have to do is practice."

And then it was dinnertime and Wednesday was over —at least for another week.

3

WALDO STAYS HOME

Waldo had a headache, a stomachache, and a sore throat—only you couldn't see anything.

"There's nothing wrong with him, Mom," said Hilary. "He just doesn't want to go to school."

Mr. Banister came into the room and looked down at the lump of Waldo curled under the quilt. "Looks like a very serious case of Monday Morning," he announced. Then he went to look for his hat, which was on his head, and when he found it he left for his office.

Mrs. Banister stood over Waldo, thermometer in hand. "Let me see your tongue," she said. Waldo groaned and stuck out a pink tongue. His mother shook the thermometer and Waldo began to protest. Temperature didn't tell everything. You could be perfectly normal and still be dying.

Hilary snickered. She fastened her hair with a clip, looked in the mirror, decided she couldn't stand the way she looked, took the clip out, put it back in again, and went to her room to change clothing.

"Hilary!" she heard her mother calling. "That's the third time you've changed. Hurry up, or you'll be late for school."

"What about *him?*" Hilary countered. "Why don't you make *him* go to school? There's nothing wrong with him. He just wants to stay home and watch television."

"Mind your own business!" screamed Waldo, starting to leap in the direction of his sister. Then remembering how sick he was, he groaned, clutched his stomach, and collapsed in bed.

"Waldo isn't going to watch television if he stays home," said Mrs. Banister primly, and Hilary knew that despite the normal temperature, Waldo would get his way. Waldo grunted, coughed, and asked for an aspirin, as if to assure his mother of her wisdom in letting him stay home.

By now Hilary had assembled her books and was ready to leave for school. She stopped in Waldo's room. "Wish me luck on the math test."

"Yeah."

"No, *say* it, stupid."

Waldo sighed. "Good luck on your math test."

"And pray for me at ten o'clock."

"I'm sick. Leave me alone," said Waldo feebly.

"WALLLdo!" Hilary threatened. One hand reached for the quilt under which Waldo had buried himself.

"O.K., O.K.," said Waldo, and with that his sister finally left him in peace and went off to school.

At ten o'clock when he was supposed to pray for Hilary's math test, Waldo lay snuggled under the warm covers, enjoying his stolen sleep. His mother had given him his breakfast, and then had left to do the marketing. "I'll double-lock the door," she had said. "Don't let anyone in."

"Don't worry, Mom," he had reassured her, for he liked staying in the house alone. There was no one to give him orders and tell him what to do. And he could sleep. A little later he was lying there not quite awake, when as if from far away he heard Hilary playing the piano. *La-di Da-di DA* . . .

In the sleepy silence of the deserted morning house, beds unmade, pillows untidy, the sound of piano music seemed out of place. He shook his head to make it go away and concentrated on sleeping. The piano had no right opening its mouth so early in the day. It was enough that in the evening he had to listen to Hilary practice.

Hey! Wait a second. Hilary was in school. He couldn't believe she'd stayed home, too.

He listened again, but the piano was silent, so he rubbed his eyes and pulled the covers over his head. But just as the dark warmth began to carry him off, the playing began again. With a start, Waldo sat up, frightened. He was alone in the house. His mother had locked the door, of course. He began to shiver at the thought of burglars, or kidnapers! Maybe he was hearing things. He shook his head and pressed the palms of his hands to his ears. He was too old to be afraid to stay alone, but maybe . . . maybe . . . Cautiously, he stepped out of bed and tiptoed into the hall. Somehow, he didn't expect to find Hilary at the piano. The playing grew louder. At the living-room door he hesitated and then peeked inside.

For Chrissakes! Waldo flew back to bed, jumped in feet first, and lay there, his heart pounding wildly. This time God had really punished him for not going to school: he was going crazy. Flipped! Or maybe he was sick—delirious, even. The living room was empty. There was no one at the piano. The keys were moving and the thing was playing itself.

For a few seconds, Waldo held his breath and willed the piano to be silent. The instrument seemed to hear him and obey. A fire engine wailed up the street outside. Inside, the house was quiet. Waldo began to calm down. Lying in bed, alert, he sent another order to the piano, commanding it to behave itself and let him enjoy his morning at home.

And then, as if mocking him, the music began again, *La-di Da-di-Da LAdi DAdi*, Hilary's piece running brightly over the keys, certainly not the way Hilary played it.

Grabbing his baseball bat, Waldo ran out of his room. "Hey, Mom! Is that you? Who's there?" he called bravely. He stepped toward the living room, and as he did, the playing stopped. This time he hid behind the door, his bare feet planted firmly on the cold floor. Later, Waldo wasn't certain why he had remained, but something held him there, as if the piano had broken off in the middle of a message.

At first, nothing happened. The grandfather clock chimed the half hour and the silent house seemed to laugh back at Waldo standing there shivering in his pajamas. He relaxed and shifted his grip on the baseball bat. Turning, he was about to start back to the bedroom when, out of the corner of his eye, he thought he saw . . . no, he *saw* a flutter of brown ragpicker dress streak down the front hall and disappear through the front door. With a bound, Waldo was back in his room, slamming the door behind him. Safe in bed, he pulled the covers over his head and lay there in the dark, breathing.

When Hilary came home from school, she was surprised to find the doctor just leaving. Waldo had the flu. He was really sick.

"I'm so glad I didn't make him go to school this morning," said Mrs. Banister. She smoothed the quilt on Waldo's bed and adjusted the shades to cut down the light. "What would you like to drink, dear?" she asked Waldo.

Waldo's eyes were closed. "Lemonade," he said in a hoarse whisper.

Hilary frowned at her brother. "I thought you hated lemonade."

"Leave him alone, Hilary. He's sick," said Mrs. Banister, for which Waldo was grateful. He didn't know why he'd asked for lemonade. He just said it.

Hilary stood at the foot of her brother's bed. "I'm sorry about this morning. I really thought you were faking. That's what you get for crying 'wolf' all those other times. You shouldn't, you know."

Waldo groaned unhappily and turned his face to the wall. Even with his eyes squeezed shut, he could still see that flash of brown ragpicker dress fleeing down the hall. What was she doing there? How could the piano play? He started to tell Hilary about it, but his throat hurt. It felt like knives were cutting into it. Suddenly, waves of nausea began to sweep over him. He lay, not daring to talk, face down in the pillow, clenching his teeth, concentrating on not moving. Maybe if he held his breath and lay perfectly still, the awful feeling would go away. As from a great distance, he heard his sister say something and then move out of the room. He wanted to call to her to come back, but his ears rang and his head reeled as if it were disconnecting from his body. And then, as the dark reached up to claim him, he fell into a sick, sweaty sleep.

Two days later Waldo was better. Every time he tried to think about the morning he got sick, he found he couldn't concentrate. Once even, he came close to telling Hilary, but the piano playing, the glimpse of ragpicker dress, that whole strange, empty morning seemed to dissolve in a haze of unreal time and feverish dreams swirling at the edge of his illness.

His mother arrived with his morning medicine and a glass of lemonade. He wrinkled his nose and made a face. "Don't you know I hate lemonade," he said.

Mrs. Banister shook her head. "Waldo," she said, "you are the strangest boy." But she took the lemonade away and brought him orange juice instead.

4

WHAT'S FOR DINNER?

A week later, Hilary was sitting on the kitchen table swinging her legs. "What's for dinner, Mom?" she asked.

"Liver, dear," said Mrs. Banister, taking a package of meat out of the refrigerator.

"Yuch!" Hilary made a face.

"Hey Mom, what's for dinner?" yelled Waldo, dashing into the kitchen.

"We're having liver," said Mrs. Banister, opening the package.

"I hate liver."

"You hate everything," said Mrs. Banister. "Hilary, please set the table."

"I always set. Why can't Waldo do it?"

"He's a boy."

"So what? He eats."

34

"Waldo takes out the garbage." Mrs. Banister dumped some flour on a plate.

"My heart's breaking."

"Waldo does other jobs around the house."

"Like what?"

"Well, he *will* when he's older."

"Yeah," piped Waldo. "I've gotta go in the army. I could get killed. Girls don't have to."

"Oh SHUT up, Mr. Know-It-All!"

"Children! Children! Stop this at once!" Mrs. Banister took a bloody-looking slab of liver and sloshed it through the flour. The liver turned white. Hilary decided it looked better—calmer—that way. She got out plates, knives, forks, spoons, and set the table.

A little later Mr. Banister came home from his office. "Hello, hello," he called. "I'm home." He gave Mrs. Banister a kiss on the top of her head and went to wash up.

"What's for dinner?" asked Mr. Banister as he took his seat at the table.

"Liver, dear," said Mrs. Banister, putting a piece on his plate.

"Please pass the ketchup," said Mr. Banister.

Hilary's father drowned everything in ketchup. Hilary couldn't understand why her mother was taking a course in French cooking. True, her mother liked to do things "nicely." She was a perfectionist, her friends said. But for their family—French cooking was about the stupidest thing Hilary could think of. Hilary hated everything except pizza and fried chicken (both bad for her skin). Waldo couldn't stand having the foods on his plate mix, which meant he never ate anything runny or wet. Mr. Banister ate ketchup. And Mrs. Banister lived on cottage cheese since she was always dieting.

During dinner Waldo brought up the matter of his allowance. Even Hilary agreed it was pathetic. In three months Waldo would be nine and his allowance would be raised from twenty-five cents to fifty cents. Big deal.

Mr. Banister helped himself to another piece of meat and doused it in ketchup. "Too much too soon—that's what's wrong with all of you," he said. "Children today think money grows on trees. When I was a boy, we worked for what we got, and when we grew up we understood the meaning of money."

"And besides," said Mrs. Banister, "if you get everything you want when you are young, there will be nothing left to look forward to when you grow up."

"How do you know I'll be alive when I grow up?" protested Waldo. "Maybe an atom bomb'll drop on me."

Hilary wondered why grown-ups could never appreciate looking forward to NOW. Her father was always talking about how great things used to be, while her mother worried about keeping you from using up the Future ahead of time.

Now, Waldo began the usual argument about how did they expect him to earn money if they wouldn't pay him for taking the garbage out and helping around the house.

"Waldo!" Mrs. Banister was shocked. She put some rice on his plate.

"Yiiiiiich!" he shrieked. "You got it in the liver! I won't eat it—it's contaminated!"

When Waldo's food was served he would take his fork and draw safety trenches around his meat and between each vegetable. As long as each food stayed in its own zone, Waldo was satisfied. Until Mrs. Banister finally limited Waldo to the same number of plates as the rest of the family, Waldo could use up all the dishes in the house just to eat his dinner.

"Waldo," said Mrs. Banister, "you are much too old for that kind of behavior."

"Face it, Mom, Waldo's mental," said Hilary. She turned to her brother. "What do you think happens when the food gets into your stomach, dope?" she asked, stabbing her fork into her meat.

"Hilary," said Mrs. Banister, "don't spear your meat. Please cut it."

"I did cut it."

"Cut it smaller. This is not a zoo."

"You'd never know," snickered Waldo.

"And Waldo, *you* may take your elbows off the table," said Mrs. Banister sternly.

"Then why are Daddy's elbows on the table?" Waldo asked with a little-boy smirk.

"Don't be fresh, Waldo. Your father's elbows are not on the table."

Mr. Banister removed his elbows from the table.

Waldo scowled. The conversation was getting stupid and his rice was flooded with brown liver juice. For some reason it reminded him of something. He couldn't think what, and then, frowning, he remembered: the brown ragpicker dress. "Did you hear what happened to Hilary with Miss Orpheo?" he asked.

"Considering how little she practices, nothing would surprise me," Mr. Banister observed. "Any child who can learn to play the piano on ten minutes twice a week must be an absolute genius."

Everyone laughed except Hilary, who was furious. Maybe it was true, but they didn't have to say it.

Hilary started to say something, but her mother said, "Don't talk with your mouth full," and so Waldo gleefully told the story of chanting the magic spell, only to have Miss Orpheo emerge from nowhere and inquire: *Have you lost something, Hilary?* Waldo imitated Miss Orpheo.

"You should have seen Hil's face," howled Waldo, doubling up with laughter.

"Hilary," said Mrs. Banister gently, "don't you think you are a little too old to believe in magic?"

"Not if it's the right kind of magic," she answered. "It certainly can't hurt. And besides," she added, "it provides psychological security. In school, we were talking about witch doctors and magicians, and Mr. Harrison told us that sometimes it doesn't make any difference whether or not something works, as long as you believe it works. 'The mind is its own magic,' he says."

"Whew!" said Mr. Banister.

"It's not silly, Dad," said Waldo. "It works, really."

Hilary smiled and shook her head at her brother. Waldo was a hopeless case. *He* even believed in God! The first blow to Hilary's religious faith had come when she discovered that the Bible was filled with jerky fairy tales about Adam and Eve and Noah's Ark. The third grade brought a worse shock. Beyond the familiar vault of the sky, where once she had supposed Heaven to be, there were endless galaxies of stars, fleeing outward through a universe whose dimensions no one could even imagine. And then one day, Hilary had simply stopped believing in God.

"The sun and the moon, clouds, magnets, and gravity," Hilary had explained to Waldo one evening when she caught him saying his prayers, "did what they did because they had *causes*. Even their causes had causes. People who believed that God was a little man stuck up in the sky who answered people's prayers were old-fashioned, soft-headed nitwits. They might as well be living in the Dark Ages when people thought angels pushed the planets through the sky."

"Did they really?" Waldo had interrupted.

"And they also believed," Hilary had told her brother, "that God put all those stars up there in the sky and one day just turned the whole thing on."

"You mean like pushing a button?"

"Yep."

"Then I guess you don't believe in Adam and Eve, either?" Waldo had asked, looking at her with large trusting eyes.

"Certainly not," was her emphatic answer. "Nor in Santa Claus, the Wizard of Oz, or the Tooth Fairy."

Waldo had been impressed by his sister's logic. Although his faith in God was shaken, it was not broken.

Deep inside, Waldo knew that God was not something you proved.

Suddenly Hilary asked, "Mom, can I quit piano? I hate it. I hate Miss Orpheo. Please, let me. Please, Mom, please?"

Hilary's father went on eating. Hilary's mother pretended to be shocked. She wasn't. They held this discussion at least once a week.

"Of course not, Hilary," said Mrs. Banister patiently. "If you stop piano lessons now, you'll . . ."

". . . be sorry when you grow up." Hilary completed the sentence. "Only I won't." The words were meaningless. She knew how she felt now; how could she feel what it would be like to feel sorry about something twenty years from now?

"Nevertheless, Hilary," continued Mrs. Banister, "you *will* be grateful later on."

"No I won't." Hilary shook her head.

Mr. Banister pushed his glasses to the top of his head so that he could see. "Your mother's right, Hilary. Someday you'll thank us for making you take piano lessons. When your mother was a child, her parents couldn't afford to give her piano lessons. You children are spoiled. You have everything."

"That's true," said Mrs. Banister. "I had to come home right after school and help my mother with the housework and look after my younger sisters."

Hilary looked at her mother. It was hard to imagine her mother working after school. Stories about her mother's childhood were like fairy tales. Hilary loved to hear them, especially when she was sick in bed, feeling too awful to read or watch television. Then she would say to her mother, "Tell me a story about when you were a little girl." Now, however, her mother looked puzzled.

"I believe you, Mom, but . . ."

"But it's true, dear—and it wasn't so long ago," her mother said, sounding hurt.

"I didn't mean to hurt your feelings—but you just don't understand."

"But I *do* understand." Mrs. Banister looked wistful. She bent over to haul Waldo out from under the table. As usual, he was trying to escape to his room before he was excused.

Hilary tried a different argument. "Well, if you've never played the piano, how do you know it's so important for me to play?"

"I know," said Mrs. Banister firmly. She plunked Waldo back into his seat.

Hilary sighed. The trouble was, every time she got angry at her mother (which these days seemed about every four and a half seconds), she'd have to face the fact that she couldn't think of any other mother she would rather have instead. At least her mother didn't seem to mind being a mother. Hilary knew she should be grateful to her parents. They were bringing her up with "Advantages." Unfortunately, Hilary's Advantages looked more like Disadvantages than anything else.

"Well," she said sulkily, "I hate Miss Orpheo. And nothing can change that! Honestly, Mom, she treats me like a baby. After all, I *am* in the sixth grade, but you'd never know it from HER. I hate her, Mom, I really do!"

"Hilary, it's not nice to hate," Mrs. Banister scolded.

Hilary could see she wasn't getting anywhere. "I hate her because she deserves to be hated. Really, Mom, you don't know how awful it is. She makes me do those sick Loosening-up Exercises—flying around the room like some goofed-up bird."

"What's this about flying?" Mr. Banister asked suddenly. He had been sitting there, stirring his coffee with the wrong end of his spoon. By the time the Banisters reached dessert, Mr. Banister was usually far off, deeply absorbed in Fascinating Ideas. "I never stop thinking," he was fond of telling his family. "Even when I seem to be doing something else, *this* . . ." (he would tap the side of his head) ". . . keeps going."

Coming from someone else, it might have sounded conceited. But it was true. Hilary's father was a famous architect. Simon Banister's houses had won many prizes and were often photographed for important magazines. Professors and art critics considered him a genius. Hilary didn't think he looked like a genius; he looked like a father—*her* father. He read the newspaper, complained about the high cost of things, and on Sunday watched The Game on television like other fathers. Each morning he went to his office neat, pressed, and shower-damp. He returned in the evening slightly frayed, his suit crushed, and his tie loose at the collar. Although Hilary admired the starched, rather handsome morning-father, the crumpled evening-father seemed a little more like her real father.

Someday, if he ever found time, Mr. Banister intended to design a house for his own family. He also planned to remodel their present apartment, which looked like a bunch of boxes, he said. Mrs. Banister said she would be happy if he would just choose drapery fabric so that she could finally get something on the dining-room windows.

Waldo had jumped into a chair. From there he leaped to the floor and began flapping around the room, re-enacting Hilary's piano lesson. "Oh Dad, you should have seen the two of them," he howled, laughing and hugging himself. He broke off suddenly, remembering what he had seen the morning he got sick. All at once, it didn't seem funny.

"I almost had a heart attack," said Hilary, turning her eyes from her brother.

"If you ask me, Miss Orpheo's the one who'll have the heart attack. She can't be that young any more," observed Mr. Banister.

"I'm certain Miss Orpheo has a reason for her methods," said Hilary's mother. "According to Martha Claxton, Miss Orpheo is an excellent teacher. You know, Martha was a very fine pianist herself, before she married Harold. I would trust Martha Claxton's judgment in musical matters any day."

"And *only* in musical matters," mumbled Hilary's father.

"Why?" asked Waldo.

"Never mind, why," said Mr. Banister.

"As I was saying," continued Mrs. Banister, "for peo-

43

ple who don't play themselves, choosing a piano teacher is risky—almost like choosing a doctor."

"Like buying a pig in a poke," volunteered Mr. Banister.

"Simon, *please,* you're not helping!" Mrs. Banister gave her husband a sharp look. "Miss Orpheo is on the staff of the Henrietta St. George Music School—one of the best schools in the city. Instead of complaining, Hilary, you should consider yourself fortunate."

"But she hates me," said Hilary, sounding miserable.

"Don't be silly, dear. Miss Orpheo doesn't hate anyone."

"How do you know?" asked Hilary.

Her mother ignored her. "You know, Hilary, she's had a very difficult life. After all, being the daughter of a great violinist like Alexander Orpheo wasn't exactly easy."

"Tell us the story of Miss Orpheo and her father," Waldo begged.

"Not now, Waldo," said Mrs. Banister. "Besides, you've heard it a hundred times."

Waldo took a sugar cube out of the sugar bowl and cracked it between his teeth. "I wonder what her house looks like?" he asked.

"Waldo! You're not a horse." Hilary pushed the sugar bowl away from her brother. "It's probably full of metronomes to pump the blood through her body, and a piano to sleep in instead of a bed." Hilary tried to picture Miss Orpheo sleeping inside a piano. It was easy. The two of them were made for each other. But what did she wear? A ragpicker nightgown? No. Miss Orpheo didn't undress. "She probably sleeps in her clothing. In her shoes, too," said Hilary rolling her eyes.

"Children!" exclaimed Mrs. Banister. "I think that's enough of this kind of discussion. That poor woman has had little enough pleasure in her life. Please clear the table. Then go and do your homework. Waldo," she scolded, "you didn't drink your milk. Do you want to get rickets?"

"Yes," said Waldo.

Mr. Banister kissed his wife, thanked her for the delicious dinner, and went into the bedroom to look at his mail. A few minutes later he reappeared, scowling. "All junk—or bills," he grumbled, as he dropped several unopened letters into the trash pail. "This one's your department, dear. The Henrietta St. George Music School. They probably want money." He handed Mrs. Banister a long envelope and walked out of the kitchen muttering, "Ads and bills . . . nobody writes letters any more."

Mrs. Banister took the letter and opened it. "Why, Hilary dear, it's an announcement of the annual piano recital at your music school."

"What recital?" Hilary asked. (As if she didn't know!)

Mrs. Banister continued reading the announcement. "How lovely, dear, you're to play in it again this year."

"Over my dead body," muttered Hilary. But nobody heard her, because she spoke the words to herself.

45

5

MAdAME St. GEORGE

Hilary sat in science class and looked at her watch: quarter to three. The classroom chatter grew louder as Mr. Harrison struggled with the science demonstration. There was a test tube clamped over a Bunsen burner, with another tube going to an upside-down collecting bottle sitting in a pan of water. The Bunsen burner hissed and glowed blue. Aside from that, nothing had happened for the past ten minutes, and the class was growing restless.

"Ah, there now." Mr. Harrison looked up from his apparatus and wiped his large forehead with the back of his arm. "You see, I have put the potassium chlorate and manganese dioxide into the test tube . . ."

Hilary watched carefully. She loved science experiments. When they worked, it was like watching a magician pull little scarves out of a walnut shell. When they didn't work, well—Mr. Harrison usually forgot to assign homework.

A paper airplane flew across the room. It worked better than the experiment. Mr. Harrison had better get it together fast, Hilary thought. Raymond Mooley and smelly Gerald were bent under their desks loading their peashooters. The Samuels twins were choking each other. And it was getting really noisy.

At last Mr. Harrison looked up, ready. The children grew quiet, waiting for the show to begin. The science teacher lifted the bottle from the pan of water, lighted a wooden splint, and waved it aloft. It went out. With a shake of his head, he picked up another splint and a match.

"I haaaate this!" Hilary's friend, Lisa, was sitting petrified, with her hands clapped over her ears and her eyes squeezed shut. "I'm so scared," she moaned.

Hilary laughed and pulled Lisa's long pigtail. "Dope, open your eyes. Nothing's happening. Besides, it's just supposed to burn brighter, not explode," she explained.

"And it won't even do that," said Cookie, who sat on the other side of Lisa. "His experiments never work."

Hilary felt sorry for the teacher. If she ever became a teacher, she'd make sure her experiments worked. She'd rehearse them forever before she'd stand up in front of a class and let them light stink bombs and things while she fussed with the equipment.

"All right, class, I think we're ready now." Mr. Harrison struck the match with a flourish and fumbled with the oxygen bottle.

Slam. Down went Lisa's head, buried in her arms. Cookie busied herself curling her long red hair around a pencil. Hilary rested her hand gently on silly Lisa's head and watched intently. Hurry, Mr. Harrison, hurry.

But just then the bell rang—loud, harsh, and final. School was over for the day. Mr. Harrison looked up, shook his head in dismay, and went back to puttering with the stubborn experiment. When it became clear he wasn't going to dismiss them, the children clattered out of their seats and fled.

Hilary wriggled into her jacket and grabbed her books. Just as she left the room, she noticed the flare burning brightly inside the oxygen bottle, but there was no one left to witness the triumph of Mr. Harrison and his invisible gas.

Out in the hall, Hilary found herself wafted along on a great three-o'clock wave of pushing, shouting students. All day they'd drifted from class to class, half awake, half alive. Now summoned back to life, they bounced down the staircase, rattling lunchboxes, jouncing schoolbags, pouring out through the school doors into the fresh air. Outside, they flooded the sidewalk in front of the building and spilled into the street where they blocked traffic. Freedom, at last.

But not for Hilary. Pushing her way through the crowd, Hilary crossed the street and looked around for Cookie. Finally, she spotted her friend's long red hair. "Hey, Cook, over here," she called. Cookie had freckles to go with the hair, glasses, and a pert, round face.

"Well, at least he forgot to give us homework," said

Play the Bach, Dear!

Cookie as she elbowed her way over to Hilary. In addition to her schoolbooks, Cookie carried a violin case.

Cookie was Hilary's best friend. They had met in the sandbox in the playground when they were little kids, and so they'd known each other since almost the beginning of their lives. The children had made sand cakes and cookies together, and Cookie had let Hilary use her pail.

"Hey, you two, we're going for pizza," Lisa yelled from across the street.

"Can't," Hilary shouted. "I've got a music lesson."

"Me, too," Cookie yelled. And together the two music students headed up the block.

Ten minutes later they were trudging down Park Avenue on their way to the Henrietta St. George Music School. Every other week Hilary went to the music school for her lesson. On alternate weeks Miss Orpheo came to Hilary's house.

Cookie's violin case banged into Hilary's leg. She shifted it to her other hand and went on explaining about her violin teacher. "Mr. Raelli is really very nice," she said. "He's always saying he thinks people should enjoy music. He doesn't believe in metronomes, and he wears sandals. Why don't you get your mother to let you switch to the violin?" Cookie suggested.

"You've got to be kidding!" Hilary snorted. "Let's face it, Cook, it takes talent to play the violin, or at least an *ear*. I couldn't even tune the thing."

"But Mr. Raelli would understand. He says we can't all be Mozart. You'd learn after a while."

"Nope. I'm hopeless."

They paused at the corner to wait for the traffic light to turn green. Half a block ahead, Hilary saw Lyra Lyons hurrying to the St. George Music School for her piano lesson.

"Look," said Hilary, pointing. "Lyra Lyons. I wonder if being fat makes you sing better?"

Cookie giggled. "Did you hear her in school yesterday?"

"Yeah." Lyra had been asked to sing at the special assembly. She sang "Where 'Er You Walk" in a rich, velvety voice, with a tragic look on her face. It was so beautiful it made Hilary tingle all over. Of course, Lyra came from a musical family. Her grandmother had been an opera singer. I guess it's just something you're born with, Hilary thought with a sigh.

The light changed and the two friends crossed the street. Cookie tried to cheer her up. "How do you know you're hopeless? Mr. Raelli says everyone can learn if they're properly taught."

"Everybody except me," said Hilary firmly. "Believe me, I know."

The two girls walked the remaining block to the music school in silence. The Henrietta St. George Music School was located on a lovely tree-lined street, in a five-story mansion that had once been a rich man's home. "Yuch. I can't bear to go in." Hilary groaned as she pulled open the heavy front door of the school.

They walked past the secretary's office, which had been

constructed by partitioning a corner of the elegant entrance hall. Miss Edgeworth, the school secretary, was busy filing her nails. A top-heavy woman with harsh, bleached-blond hair and thick brown eyebrows, Miss Edgeworth sat at her typewriter and, whenever the phone rang, sang into it, "Henrietta St. George Music School —may I help you?"

"I can't take her," Hilary whispered to Cookie.

"Yeah, I know what you mean. She's such a phony."

Miss Edgeworth was all sweetness and light if you were cute and adorable, or, let's face it, if you really belonged in the Henrietta St. George Music School. But if you were nobody, an outsider, like Hilary Banister, and you came to Miss Edgeworth's desk to ask if anybody had found a green glove, or whether your mother had left a message saying where she was meeting you after your lesson, the secretary would look right through you as if you were invisible. On the other hand, she had no trouble seeing teachers, visitors (especially men), and always had a warm greeting for her favorite pupils.

Hilary and Cookie hung their jackets in the coatroom and left their books on a shelf. The coatroom had once been a closet, according to Hilary's father, who knew everything about all the old mansions in the city. Hilary was impressed by a closet so large that people could use it as a room. Two girls were laughing and talking. A boy with Brillo hair was sitting on a bench, writing in a music notebook. Several other students hurried in and out of the room chatting gaily. An eight-year-old child prodigy, accompanied by her doting mother, arrived for her lesson. For a moment the room grew silent. Word had gotten around. Everyone turned to stare at the little kid. The child prodigy didn't seem to mind.

"C'mon, let's get out of here," said Hilary. Cookie took her violin and they left.

As they passed the recital hall; they could hear Madame Fluchnagel and Mr. Spedorio conducting an opera rehearsal. Mr. Spedorio began shouting in Italian. Then Madame Fluchnagel began yelling in some other language. The recital hall had once been the ballroom of the mansion. The beautiful parquet floor had been made of polished oak, according to Mr. Banister. A magnificent crystal chandelier had hung from the ceiling, glittering above the heads of dancers whirling beneath, and a wall of vast, arching windows had looked out on the garden below. Now the floor was covered with drab gray carpeting. The hand-carved moldings and wood paneling had been stripped and sold to antique dealers. The room was clogged with metal folding chairs, and the windows were hung with mud-colored drapes.

The girls climbed the stairs to the lesson rooms on the third and fourth floors. Two boys came jumping down the stairs, three steps at a time, and almost knocked them over. When the heavy oak doors of the lesson rooms were closed, the school was remarkably quiet. But each time a door opened, bursts of music would spill out, flooding the old building with sound. A string quartet, bent over gleaming instruments, practiced in the second-floor conservatory. Somewhere upstairs, a high soprano was practicing scales and arpeggios.

All the rich, warm sounds, Hilary thought, of music students who knew what they were doing, who *belonged* in the school. All this had nothing to do with Hilary Banister, she told herself. She was not part of it.

Every other week in a music room furnished with two grand pianos, a green blackboard, and an ashtray stuck on a tall stand, Hilary played her dinky little pieces. *One-and, 2-and, 3-and, 4 . . . I can't stand you any more!* Tick, tick went the metronome. No! No! went Miss Orpheo. If anyone had opened the door to Hilary's lesson room, the music trickling outside would have sounded plinkety plink plink: a child's notes, thin, uncertain, and labored; nothing like the brilliant cascades of notes or the glorious singing tones that came from the other rooms.

Hilary and Cookie parted on the third floor. Cookie continued upstairs. Hilary moved down the hall until she came to her lesson room. The door was closed. Her eyes darted to the left, to the right. Good. No one was coming. Pressing her hands together, she bowed her head, squeezed her eyes shut, and hastily whispered the Piano-lesson Spell. It wasn't the proper way to do it, Hilary knew. But it was better than nothing. Besides, saying the spell had become a habit.

She pushed the hair out of her face, opened the door, and went in. Miss Orpheo, in a gray ragpicker dress, was waiting for her. Miss Orpheo owned ragpicker dresses in colors ranging from bilious-blue and grim-gray to gravy-brown and no-color. Once, when Hilary's mother was trying to determine just what it was that Hilary detested about the piano teacher, Hilary had tried to explain the ragpicker dresses. Her mother was shocked. "Dear, that's not nice. It's unkind." "Well, it's depressing, and it makes her look like those people who shop in trash pails," Hilary had said.

While Hilary settled her music on the piano, Miss Orpheo reached for the metronome. She clutched the instrument to herself and wound it hard. She seemed to be winding herself up. For what? Hilary wondered. To give a piano lesson? Next, Miss Orpheo moved to the window, and again Hilary had the fleeting sensation that the light from the street was passing right through Miss Orpheo's thin frame.

"Hilary," said Miss Orpheo, "I think it is time to plan your program for the piano recital in December. It will be here before we know it."

Hilary took a deep breath. "I don't want to play in the recital!" There, she'd said it.

"You don't want to play in the recital?" echoed Miss Orpheo. She wheeled around and faced Hilary. "Why, that's absurd! Everybody plays in the recital. Madame St. George expects you to, your parents expect . . ."

"That's the whole point," Hilary interrupted. "My father said after the last concert he wouldn't be caught dead at another one of those things. My brother says it's bad enough to have to listen at home."

Miss Orpheo's eyes narrowed. "But your mother . . ." she said almost hopefully. "I am certain she would be terribly disappointed if you did not play."

"Oh, my mother," said Hilary bitterly. How could she make Miss Orpheo understand? "All she cares about is being able to drag me out when they're having company and, you know . . ." Hilary mimicked her mother's voice: *"Hilary dear, Aunt Ottilie and Uncle Archer* haven't heard you play in so long. Wouldn't you like to play a little something for them? If I say I wouldn't like to, they rub it in, saying that after all the money they've spent on piano lessons, you'd think it wouldn't be asking too much to expect me to be able to play SOME-THING. And then if I do play," Hilary continued resentfully, "they don't listen."

Miss Orpheo frowned. Her reply was interrupted by a sharp knock on the door.

"May I come in?" called Madame St. George in a rasping voice, whereupon the door opened and the director of the music school swept into the room. Miss Orpheo smoothed her dress with the palms of her hands and rushed to greet her.

Henrietta St. George, the founder of the school that bore her name, was an enormous woman who looked like a grand piano and possessed the iron will of an orchestra of pianos. She spoke eight languages, all badly, sometimes all at once. She had a great long nose, with two sharp creases on each side, all pointing downward. Her mouth went down, her chin went down, her bosom went down. Down, down, all down. She was also deaf—or so it was rumored. She wore a hearing aid which she adjusted so that she heard only what she wanted to hear. Hilary hated her.

"Why, Madame St. George! How kind of you to drop in on us." Miss Orpheo sounded nervous. "Hilary and I were just discussing the pieces she is to prepare for the recital." Miss Orpheo fixed Hilary with her eyes, but avoided looking directly at Madame St. George.

Play the Bach, Dear!

Hilary sat at the piano, scowling, cursing, staring into her lap.

"Hilary's been learning a Chopin Mazurka. We thought we'd do that," Miss Orpheo announced, "and perhaps a movement from the Mozart C-major Sonata. You know the Mazurka . . . LA li-la-li la-li pum-ti PUM . . ." Miss Orpheo's voice soared. She stopped abruptly, embarrassed. Miss Orpheo had a surprisingly un-Orpheolike voice, Hilary realized.

Madame St. George waved her arms at Hilary. "*Merveilleux!*" she cried. "The Chopin is such a lovely thing." She turned to Miss Orpheo, ". . . and . . . er . . . technically not too difficult. As I always remind my students: Beauty and Simplicity—they go together," by which Hilary knew Madame St. George meant that the Mazurka was so easy even a musical moron could play the thing.

"Perhaps it would be wiser not to do the Mozart, though," cautioned Madame St. George, looking directly at Miss Orpheo. She fiddled with her hearing aid and lowered her voice. "Some of the others are planning to do it . . . the von Mess child, I believe." She gave Miss Orpheo a condescending smile which Hilary translated: You'd do better not to compete with this one.

Hilary felt a little sorry for Miss Orpheo. Arabella von Mess was Mrs. Tarsatini's pupil. She was about nine years old and wore dresses her grandmother knitted for her. Another genius. The Henrietta St. George School reeked with geniuses. The most talented pupils usually went to Mr. André or to Mrs. Tarsantini. Everyone agreed Mr. André was a very fine musician and an excellent

teacher. According to Miss Orpheo, however, "the Tarsatini woman" was another matter. She played like a machine! That was all Hilary had ever been able to get
Miss Orpheo to say on the subject. Was Miss Orpheo
jealous?

Madame St. George was a formidable woman. Even
Miss Orpheo seemed timid in her presence. But Hilary
was beginning to feel desperate.

"Madame St. George," she said softly, "I don't think
. . . I mean, if you don't mind, I'd rather not play at
the recital this year." And then, anticipating the next
question, she added, "I just don't want to."

"Speak up, child," Madame St. George screeched, tap-
ping her hearing aid.

Hilary said it again.

"*Mon dieu!*" exploded Madame St. George. "*Not* par-
ticipate in our recital! I have never heard such nonsense.
Have *you*, Miss Orpheo?"

Miss Orpheo pressed her thin lips together and shook
her head. She had turned very pale.

Frantically, Hilary hunted for a suitable excuse. She
could never tell them she didn't want to play because
she hated the dark, frightening recital hall and all the
bratty children, each trying to play louder and faster
than the other. She hated the snob-parents who came
only to hear their own little darlings, who talked and
fidgeted through the rest of the recital. It was bad
enough to know you'd never get out on the stage without tripping over your feet, but to be eleven years old,
in the sixth grade, and to be outplayed by some little

kid only half your age was humiliating. For once, she hated being tall. She felt like a big, stupid gawk.

"Hilary suffers from stage fright," Miss Orpheo apologized. "I was about to assure her that she will get over it." The piano teacher stood behind the piano, her hands spread on the top, gripping, as if for support. She thought for a moment. "Everyone gets nervous playing in public," she said. "We must go out on the stage, Hilary, and pretend that we cannot be seen, that we are alone with the piano."

"I'll never get over it," said Hilary stubbornly.

Throwing her head back, Madame St. George loosed a torrent of laughter which came tumbling down three octaves of the scale, wiping out everything in its path. Then crossing her arms in front of her vast sloping bosom, she peered down at Hilary.

"Stage fright, did you say? Ha! That is nothing." She flung her arms through the air, dismissing the stage fright. "The great Josef Lhevinne suffered from such terrible stage fright, they practically had to push him out on the stage. And Paderewski . . . before a concert . . . the noble, the sublime Paderewski, ah! A pathetic sight. He too, they pushed."

Hilary had heard these stories before. Miss Orpheo had told her about Josef Lhevinne, a fabulous pianist with a flawless technique. Once, in the middle of a concert, he suddenly forgot what he was supposed to play next. So what? When Josef Lhevinne, Paderewski, Horowitz, or any of the other nervous geniuses finally got out on the stage, they could PLAY. People applauded. The concert had a happy ending. Hilary's recital would have no such happy ending. She was certain of that.

Madame St. George moved toward the door. It was settled. "Of course you shall play. It is good experience." She turned for a moment, her hand resting on the doorknob. "Forgive me for taking your time, Miss Orpheo—and don't do the Mozart," she added. "*Au revoir!*" With that, she sailed out of the room, closing the door on Hilary, on Miss Orpheo—in fact, on the entire subject.

The rest of the hour was miserable. Hilary was so upset, she left out sharps, mixed up pedaling, and got lost in her scales. The Bach Invention, still littered with old mistakes, broke out in enough fresh mistakes to compose an entire new piece. Poor Bach. Poor Chopin. Poor Hilary Banister.

6

IN THE PARK

Rrrrring! Hilary made a dive for the phone. It was Cookie. Could Hilary go to the park with her?

"Wait. I'll ask my mother."

Mrs. Banister was dressing to go out. "Well, I don't know," she hesitated. "Stevie came over to play with Waldo for the afternoon. I suppose it will be all right, if you take the two boys with you." Mrs. Banister looked at her new dress in the mirror and frowned. "Don't go too far, Hilary," she added, "and stay where there are people. And please be home by five," she called as Hilary dashed back to the phone.

"We've got to drag *them*." Hilary doodled a picture of a naked lady on the telephone pad. She made long hair and added a hat. "Yeah, I suppose you're right. It's better than nothing." Leave it to Cookie to be practical.

She didn't get so worked up about things. Of course, Cookie could afford to be generous about other people's little brothers: she was an only child.

Later, in the park, Hilary and Cookie lay sprawled on the grass. Cookie was weaving leaf crowns from the brittle oak leaves that had fallen to the ground. The boys had gone off to find a tree to climb. Hilary discussed her mother's theory.

"According to my mother," she explained, "I'm allowed to go to the park alone, providing I don't go *alone*. She thinks if there are enough of us, then nothing can happen."

"My mother doesn't care," said Cookie, dropping her head back to feel the warm autumn sun on her face.

It was true, Hilary thought. In a way, Cookie was lucky. Her parents were very permissive. That wasn't even the word for it! They didn't seem like parents at all. Cookie was allowed to go downtown on the subway and come home after dark—which in winter was practically in the middle of the afternoon. Hilary had to be home before dark. As for the subway—well, forget it.

And yet somehow, Hilary was glad her mother was *her* mother. She was glad her mother didn't let her go to the park without a bunch of other kids, and didn't let her come home from places after dark. If you knew you could go to the park alone—then you sort of *had* to.

"Oh damn!" said Cookie, interrupting Hilary's thoughts. "My crown broke." She crumpled the leaves and started over.

Hilary lay on her back and gazed over her shoulder at the lime-green slopes and the pale-blue sky, bleached in the autumnal haze. Viewed from this position, grass, bushes, and trees seemed to run downhill until they emptied into a vast lake of sky. A bird, coasting down the sky, appeared for a moment and disappeared. Above, where no bird could fly—moving swift and straight, but without the curve and swoop of the living bird—an airplane cut across the blue and vanished. In the distance, someone was playing a saxophone. Otherwise, the park was unusually quiet.

Hilary loved this part of the park. If you blotted out the towers of the city skyline, and ignored the flip-top lids and the broken glass; if you sat where you couldn't see the iron lampposts, the wire litter baskets, and the curse-scribbled asphalt walks, then, looking past the stand of gnarled trees, beyond the outcrop of glacial rock, across the meadow, and up the long, sunlit slopes, you could forget it was a public park that belonged to the City of New York and pretend it was a vast, rolling estate, all your own. There were times when it was good to make believe you owned the park.

"Hey, look at me!" Waldo's voice rang out suddenly. "C'mon up, Stevie. It's real cool here." Waldo had found his tree, a prickly-looking pine, and had climbed to the top of it.

Hilary lifted herself to her elbows. She couldn't see her brother, but the tree was shaking and swaying unnaturally, and she could hear his idiotic giggles. "Waldo Banister," she called, "you'd better come down from there before you get killed!"

"I'm never coming down," sang Waldo from inside the tree. "And I won't get killed."

"Hey, Waldo, save a branch for me," shouted Stevie.

"I'm coming up, too." Stevie had to copy everything Waldo did. Compared with drippy-nosed Stevie, Waldo was perfection. Now the tree really began to rustle and shake. Hilary was worried.

"Hey, Mr. Smarty-pants," she yelled at her brother. "What if a branch breaks?"

"I'll catch on to another. Hey, Stevie, come up this way—here, through the back." Stevie was having trouble getting off the ground.

Horrible snapping sounds were coming from the tree. Hilary didn't think her parents would appreciate it if their only son committed suicide from the top of a tree. She shook her head and lay back on the grass. "You know what that nutty kid does at home? He plays 'Mabel, Mabel, Horse's Stable.'"

"And WHAT is *that?*"

"An obstacle-course game he invented."

"I see," said Cookie, who didn't.

"One day," Hilary explained, "the kitchen floor had just been waxed, and no one was supposed to walk on it. Waldo wanted to get some potato chips, so he figured out how to get to the kitchen closet without stepping on the floor. After that it became a game."

"What does he do—fly?" asked Cookie.

"Worse. He climbs up on the washing machine, into the sink, across the stove, even on top of the fridge. And all the time he sings this crazy song he made up:

> *'Mabel, Mabel, horse's stable,*
> *Catch me, catch me, if you're able.'*"

"Wow!" said Cookie. "Does your mother let him?"

"Oh no. She has hysterics every time he does it."

Hilary flicked a blade of grass at Cookie. "Of course, my father thinks Waldo's very creative," she continued. "But you know my father—he's a bug on problem-solving. He's always saying you have to have an open mind in order to solve difficult problems. Sometimes the craziest ideas turn out to be just what you need, he says."

Cookie took a hank of her red hair and held it under her nose like a mustache. "Say, Hil, is it true about that last house your father designed—you know, the one that won the prize. Does it really *tilt?*"

"Yep. You saw it in that magazine. There's a panel with a set of controls. You press different buttons and the house tips north, east, south, or west."

"Yeah, I know. But, Hil, I don't get it. Why would anybody want a house that stands on a pedestal and tilts?"

"I guess there are some people who want things just because nobody else has them." Hilary had once heard her father say that to someone who asked him the same question.

Cookie nodded. It made sense. Then she thought of something. "How come your house isn't special? It's nice and all," she added hastily, "but it's like any other apartment, if you know what I mean."

"I know," Hilary agreed. "My mother's always yelling about that. She wants to know when my father is going to do something about our living room. He keeps saying he'll do it *one of these days*. My mother says, 'One of these days is none of these days.'"

Hilary was making a bird. She picked a long, thick blade of grass and tied a knot in it for the head. She attached a second piece for the wings and, holding it, zoomed the bird through the air.

"What are you going to do about the recital?" Cookie asked finally. "It's the week after Thanksgiving."

"I don't know," said Hilary, digging a hole in the ground with a stick. She was going to put the bird in it. "But I'd rather die than play in another recital."

"You could play hooky. Just not turn up . . . hide out here in the park, or something."

Hilary shook her head. "My mother'd kill me."

"You could get sick," suggested Cookie.

"*Could* get sick! I'm going to *be* sick!" Hilary cried. "Anyway, they'd still make me play. I'd have to have a burst appendix, or quadruple pneumonia . . ."

A gust of wind tangled in the treetops. Hissing out through the leaves, it set the low-hung branches dipping and swaying. Abruptly, the wind died and it was quiet again.

After a moment Cookie said, "Well, I suppose you'll just have to play. Maybe it won't be too bad."

"Are you kidding? Have you forgotten last year's piano recital?"

"Uh-uh. I wasn't there, remember? I had the flu. Was it bad?"

"HORRIBLE," Hilary groaned. "The most ghastly experience of my life."

"What happened?"

"Everything."

Hilary began to describe the music recital to Cookie, shuddering even now as she relived the events of that hideous afternoon.

She saw herself sitting in the first row of the gloomy tomb of a recital hall, alone and terrified. An enormous, ebony-black grand piano dominated the empty stage like an execution block. Anyone unworthy who dared to sit before it and touch its brilliant white keys was doomed. If you faltered, if you were unprepared . . . crunch! crunch! . . . the piano would gnash its keys and devour you immediately.

Hilary leaned back, as if to put some distance between herself and the still painful events unreeling in her head. Then she continued.

Her stomach had been doing trampoline drops. Her legs had turned to sponge, and her mouth was lined with felt. Even worse, her cold, clammy hands had trembled so violently that at any moment Hilary had expected them to break loose and run away. She had clasped her hands, one in the other, hoping they would calm and comfort each other. You can't play the piano with frightened hands.

"It's hard enough when your hands belong to you," Hilary explained to Cookie, "but like *that* . . . forget it!"

"I know what you mean," Cookie said sympathetically. "When I get nervous, my glasses fog over and my hands get sweaty. It just pours over the fingerboard of my fiddle. I feel like I'm playing in a swamp."

Again Hilary paused, overcome by the feelings of that awful afternoon. The other children had sat there chattering and squirming in their seats, self-conscious in their party clothes, nervous as high-strung horses. Hilary knew nobody and nobody knew her. She had tried saying something friendly to the thin, arty-looking girl in the seat next to her. The girl said, "Mmm," and turned around to talk to the boy on her other side. Lyra Lyons didn't talk to anybody, either. Lyra Lyons didn't have to. She thrived on recitals, on music and applause.

Hilary remembered being tempted to run right out of the recital hall and keep running until she and the Henrietta St. George Music School were in separate cities—separate COUNTRIES. Just then it had grown quiet, and Madame St. George rose to welcome her guests to a "little family musicale."

"Did she make you go through that awful lot-drawing ceremony?" Cookie asked. "I hate that."

"*You* hate it!" Hilary cried. "Wait till you hear what happened. 'In order to be fair to the children,' Madame St. George had announced, 'it is our custom to draw lots to determine the order in which the children are to perform. We meet this afternoon, not in the spirit of competition, but in the spirit of music.'" Hilary caught Madame St. George's snooty tremulo with such deadly accuracy that Cookie broke up with laughter.

"There were eighteen children," said Hilary. "Miss Edgeworth brought a glass fishbowl filled with little slips of paper. And that's when I knew! I didn't even have to look at my number. Number eighteen! Last! Condemned to sit through seventeen performances, slowly dying. By the time my turn came, I knew I wouldn't even remember what I was supposed to play."

Serena Lang went first. She flew up the steps to the

stage, hitched the piano seat beneath her, ripped through her pieces, and dashed back to her seat, flushed, and smiling with relief as the audience burst into spirited applause.

A little child whose feet barely reached the pedal played next. She looked about seven, although Hilary decided her babyish dress made her look younger than she was. The little creep minced out on the stage, settled herself at the piano, and then smiling sweetly at the audience, plunged into an angry modern composition with ninety million notes and ferocious chords. The piece ended with a crash, as if the composer suddenly decided he couldn't stand it any more. The applause was tremendous. No one would ever hear the end of "that adorable little child, no bigger than a minute." The little creep!

Adrian Scorn was announced. A hush fell over the recital hall. When Adrian played you listened because the music was beautiful, not because you got a kick out of seeing a little kid pull off something sensational—for a little kid. Adrian played the piano. With the other children, you had the feeling the piano was playing *them*.

The afternoon wore on. "Slowly, horribly, the truth began to dawn on me," Hilary said earnestly to Cookie. "Seventeen children were going to walk out on that stage and play. Then, after seventeen perfect performances, I—Hilary Banister—would have the horrible privilege of spoiling the record."

Cookie groaned, "I know what you mean. I have this thing I call 'my mistake.' I can't relax until I've made it."

"Only," said Hilary, "I had a feeling it would be

something worse than a little mistake." She went on with her story.

Disaster was inevitable. She might stumble, land on a wrong chord, go blank . . . *Where* and *how* it would happen were still to be decided. But it would happen. She was positive of that. And there she would be, in front of everybody: disgraced. Just thinking about it made her heart pound so violently, she was convinced people in the audience could hear it. She wanted to die. In a sweat, she tried to finger the opening notes of her sonatina. Nothing came. What would she do if she got up there and couldn't remember *anything!*

The audience grew restless. Children fidgeted in their seats. Somebody's little brother fell off his seat and began to cry. Suddenly, out of a dream, Hilary heard Madame St. George call her name.

Hilary had no idea how she got up on the stage, but she was well into the second line of the music before she realized that her hands had begun playing without waiting for a signal from her. The piano bench was too far away. She rocked in her seat, trying to get the bench to move, but it was too heavy. Her stomach had stopped doing flip-flops. But her hands! Ice-cold, flappy things! They hurried along the keys, dangerously out of control. They didn't belong to her. They didn't even belong to themselves.

Despite everything, she kept going. And that was the whole trouble. The longer she played without landing in serious trouble (there had been several near-misses), the sooner it had to happen. She almost wished it would happen so she could get it over with. She had the odd sensation that her fingers were considering the same thing. They began to stiffen, as if they didn't want to go on, knowing only too well what was going to happen.

She came to the part where the main theme repeated. Oh no! She missed the E-flat in the right hand and, to her horror, found herself starting over again. She was so shaken that she played on, barely conscious of what she was doing. If you didn't know the music, you might not have noticed that anything was wrong. But Hilary knew. She knew something even more awful: It could happen again!

What if she missed the E-flat again? What if she could never find her way out of the piece and had to sit there and play forever? Or until the audience finally caught the horrible joke and laughed itself sick? By now, Hilary barely knew what she was doing. Her fingers slithered around on the keys. She missed a note in a run. She fumbled a chord. She missed . . . Oh damn! Her unhappy fingers snarled, hesitated, and as she faltered, the memorized pattern began to slip from her. Desperately, her fingers fluttered over the keys, trying to regain the feeling of the notes, groping . . .

And then, you wouldn't believe what happened.

"Take your time, child," screeched Madame St. George. The woman came clumping up onto the stage, fiddling with her hearing aid, cackling, "There's no need to be nervous. We are all friends." Resting her heavy hand on Hilary's shoulder, right there in front of everybody, she went on clucking, "Tch, tch . . . you must not be upset. It can happen to anyone." (Only it didn't.) "Take it from . . . la dadi Da." And she began to sing the passage.

That did it! Once interrupted, all was lost. It had been a nasty stumble, but Hilary might have gotten the piece moving again if Madame St. George hadn't stolen it from her. Hilary's hands hovered above the keys, and in those few critical seconds the music evaporated, vanishing from her head and her fingers. A moment earlier the audience had been ready to go home. Now it became deathly quiet. Everyone stared and waited.

Hilary struggled to hold back the tears of rage that flooded her eyes. She clamped her teeth down on the inside of her cheek, biting hard. It was *her* hassle. Why hadn't they left her alone. She'd have made it.

"Take your time, Hilary," Madame St. George croaked again, making certain no one missed the point.

Hilary wanted to put her head down, let the sobs out of her throat and drown the whole piano. Everybody was watching: her family, parents, teachers, all the bratty kids . . . Writhing with anguish and embarrassment, she fumbled for the lost notes, for *any* notes that would get her through the piece, off the stage, and out of the Henrietta St. George Music School. Forever. Eventually, she got the sonatina started again, and by some miracle finished it. After that everything was a big blur.

There was a long silence when Hilary finished her story.

"How awful!" said Cookie, finding her voice finally. "No wonder you don't want to play this year. I'd die if that ever happened to me."

Hilary had gotten so excited while describing the recital that without realizing it, she'd been pulling up grass, piling it in little heaps. With a sweep of her hand she scattered the grass. "You know, it was strange. I knew all along something would happen. The more it didn't happen, the more I knew it would. It's spooky, really." Hilary lay back with her arms under her head and stared up at the vast, floating sky. There was so much of it. It was a good thing it stayed up there, she thought.

Cookie wiped her glasses on her shirt sleeve. "But this year it would be different. It couldn't happen twice. So you'd be safe."

"No," said Hilary firmly. "Don't you understand? That's the whole point. With my luck, it *will* happen again—just because it shouldn't."

Waldo came swinging down from his tree. "Was Hilary telling you about the recital last year?" he yelled. He raced to a sliding stop and dropped to his knees in front of the girls. Stevie, dirty, scratched, and grass-stained, tumbled in behind him.

"Hey, watch out! You're breaking my crown," scolded Cookie, edging away from the boys.

"You're lucky you weren't there," said Waldo, still breathing hard.

Cookie ignored him.

"What a fiasco!" continued Waldo. He grabbed a handful of dead leaves and grass and dumped it over Stevie's head.

"Hey, cut it out," yelled Stevie, brushing the stuff out of his hair.

Play the Bach, Dear!

"I told Mom if you play again this year, I'm not going," said Waldo. "It's too embarrassing."

"Thanks for the vote of confidence," Hilary muttered.

"You're welcome."

"Oh, shut up."

A shower of leaves fell from the trees and swept along the ground. The sun disappeared behind a flock of wind-driven clouds. Suddenly, the shadow of approaching winter moved across the park.

"It's getting late, we'd better be going." Hilary shivered and stood up.

Cookie dropped the crown she had just finished on the grass. Leaf crowns fell apart if you tried to take them home.

"Hey, lemme jump on it!" yelled Waldo.

"LemME break it up!" screamed Stevie.

"Just leave it," snapped Cookie. "You don't have to destroy everything you can't take with you. Maybe somebody else will find it."

Waldo stuck out his tongue. Stevie Copycat stuck out his tongue. Then the boys jumped on each other and began to roll around in the grass, all legs and arms, and little-boy shrieks.

Without the sun, the park looked bleak and lonely. Hilary and Cookie buttoned their sweaters and, calling the boys to follow, started for home.

As they emerged from the park, it suddenly grew darker. The tall buildings lining the city streets blocked the late afternoon light, depriving city people of a part of the day still enjoyed by soaring birds, airplanes, and penthouses high at the top of the city. A chill wind from the river rushed up the long canyon of buildings, caught in the girls' long hair, tangled, and whipped on. The boys raced ahead.

"I can see your point about not playing in the recital," said Cookie, brushing the hair out of her eyes. "But what are you going to do if they make you?"

"I'll think of something," Hilary promised, squeezing her eyes shut to avoid a nasty spray of dust. In a hurry now to get home, they jogged down the block. Hilary heard her father's words: *Sometimes the craziest ideas turn out to be* . . . When they caught up to the boys, they slowed to a walk.

"You could always drown yourself," suggested Cookie, puffing.

"Don't be stupid, Cookie. I can swim."

"You could tie a big rock to your legs," Waldo offered.

"Thanks, I'll remember you in my will," said Hilary.

"Me too," shrieked Stevie, hop-skipping backward in front of them. "I'd help with the rock."

Hilary glared at Stevie with disgust. Yuch. Stevie was too much. He was practically Waldo's shadow—which proved what a dope Stevie was.

"I don't know what I'm going to do," she said to Cookie, "but I'll think of something." What she needed was nothing less than a miracle.

And then they were home.

7

Awful Sunday

A wasted Sunday was about the saddest thing in the world. One certain way to ruin Sunday was to spend it cleaning up your room, doing homework, and practicing the piano. And that's exactly what Hilary was doing.

"Definitely not," said Mrs. Banister when Hilary asked if she could go over to Cookie's house for the rest of the afternoon. "After you've finished your room, you have to practice." She glanced at her watch. "By that time it will be too late."

"But, Mom," Hilary pleaded, "they're expecting me. Lisa and Ellen are there. It's the only time our committee can get together to work on our social studies report." On Friday they had all gone to Woolworth's to buy make-up. Everybody was supposed to bring her stuff, and Lisa, who had learned from her older sister, was going to show them how to do their eyes. Hilary just had to go.

"I'm afraid, Hilary," said Mrs. Banister crossly, "you should have thought of your social studies report sooner. You've had the whole weekend, and you still haven't touched the piano . . ."

"I practiced yesterday," said Hilary indignantly.

"I don't consider *that* practicing," replied her mother. "Ten minutes at the most."

Why was it, Hilary wondered, that ten minutes at the piano seemed like ten years?

"Did you clean up your room?" Mrs. Banister inquired. "It's an absolute disgrace."

"Uh-huh."

Mrs. Banister went in to inspect. Hilary followed. Mrs. Banister nodded approvingly. The room looked very neat. Very neat, indeed. She walked over to the closet. Hilary closed her eyes. The door was stuck. Mrs. Banister pulled. She pulled harder and ducked just in time. Sssswooosh . . . thump, crash, bang, KLONK! The entire closet came pouring out: boxes, games, shoes, pocketbooks, paper, notebooks, magic markers, sneakers, tennis balls, plastic straws, chess pieces, EVERY-THING. It showered beads, it rained Monopoly money, it hailed jacks. Mrs. Banister almost got hit on the head by the Chinese checkers game Hilary had tried to stuff up on the top shelf. The metal box crashed to the floor, splattering marbles, which rolled out in all directions under the furniture. It ended with a tremendous avalanche of comic books.

"Hey, what's going on?" yelled Waldo, running into

the room. He took one look at his mother's face and ran right out again.

When the dust and clatter had finally settled, Mrs. Banister looked hard at Hilary and said, "When you have finished practicing, you may clean up this incredible mess."

May clean up, Hilary echoed. *May* clean up . . . ! But there was no point arguing when her mother got like that.

Hilary shuffled toward the living room and the piano. Grown-ups were lucky. Nobody told them what to do. She couldn't wait to grow up and run her own life.

In the living room, she found her father and another man examining a set of architectural plans. Her father's clients occasionally came to the house to discuss business. Hilary was about to back out of the room when her father looked up and noticed her.

"Go right ahead, Hilary, if you want to practice. You won't bother us."

"No, it's O.K. I'll wait till later," said Hilary eagerly.

"C'mon, Simon, let the kid practice. We can go in the study and finish," said the client.

Hilary's father nodded and began collecting his papers, stuffing things into his briefcase. "There you are, Hilary. It's all yours," he said generously. "I have a feeling your mother wants you to practice now. We won't hear you inside, so don't worry."

Hilary bit her tongue. She didn't intend to worry.

Mr. Client looked at Hilary and smiled. "You're lucky your kid *plays*," he said to Hilary's father. "At least you got something for your money. Mine quit after a year.

Took up guitar. Quit that too. I paid over two thousand dollars for the piano, and another hundred for the guitar. Then lessons . . . And all for what? It cost me close to three grand to hear him play 'The Happy Farmer.'" The man laughed at his joke.

He had dandruff, Hilary noticed. She glared at him. If there was one thing she hated, it was being called "kid."

"Now, Simon, as you were saying—about the house not having any closets—" Mr. Client clapped Hilary's father on the shoulder. "I'm afraid my wife wouldn't go for that. It's tempting, all right. Might keep her from buying all those new shoes and dresses."

"Well, Henry," said Mr. Banister, laughing, "that's not exactly what I had in mind."

What it was her father had in mind, Hilary was not to know, because the two men, laughing and ha-ha-ing in their big bass voices, had moved off to the study, leaving her alone with the piano.

Hilary sat down at the piano and began clattering through an old piece, playing at top speed, hacking and whacking the notes. "I hate it . . . I hate it . . . I hate it."

"Hilary!" It was her mother at the door. "You don't mind, dear, if we close the door. Aunt Ottilie just dropped in and the noise gives her a headache." Mrs. Banister closed the double French doors quietly, shutting Hilary into the room.

Actually, Hilary did mind. If your own family couldn't bear to listen to you, then what was the use?

Hilary stood up, took a book from the bookcase and set it on top of her music. Then she settled down to reading *Fossil in the Frigidaire* (a juicy mystery), while practicing the C-major scale with her right hand. Slowly, over and over again, five octaves up the piano, and five octaves down. Once in a while, she would zoom off a bit of real music. Then back to *Fossil* and the C-major scale—left hand this time.

It was lonely at the piano. Hilary wondered what Waldo was doing. It was Sunday afternoon and everyone else in the world was having fun. Cookie, Ellen, and Lisa would be trying their eye stuff without her. And here she sat, practically chained to the piano, condemned to practice until her hands dropped off. She turned the page of her book.

Bounce! Bounce! The doors opened and a basketball came dribbling into the room, followed by Waldo. Bounce! BOUNCE! Waldo was working hard, weaving around the room behind his ball.

"You're not supposed to play ball in the house," said Hilary.

"You're not supposed to read while you're practicing." Thoomp-THOOMP! Waldo was in love with basketball. Last year it was baseball. Sports! That's all boys ever thought about. It was sickening.

"Who rang the doorbell before?" she asked.

"Just Aunt Ottilie." The ball bounced onto the coffee table and off again.

"She probably came to show off the new diamond necklace Uncle Archer gave her," said Hilary. "I heard Mom talking about it."

"Yeah." The ball hit the rug and finally died. Picking it up, Waldo twirled the ball expertly between his fingers, started it bouncing again, and departed.

The telephone rang in the hall outside. Hilary's heart

leaped. Rescue! Maybe it was for her. She waited. Any minute her mother would come through the door and call her to the phone.

"Hil-a-REEE!" her mother's voice called. "Go on with your practicing. It's not for you."

Waldo had left the living-room doors open. Aunt Ottilie stuck her head in. "Why Hilary dear, what a surprise! I thought it was Waldo playing. Oh, that's right, I forgot," continued Aunt Ottilie in a syrupy voice, "Waldo doesn't play, does he?"

Stung, Hilary felt like saying, "No, Waldo doesn't play . . . and as you may have noticed, neither do I." She ground her teeth instead, and stared at Aunt Ottilie's necklace. It was wild. It looked like a whole Junglegym crawling up her neck.

Aunt Ottilie moved into the room, followed by Hilary's mother. "Actually, I'm surprised to find you home on Sunday, Hilary dear," said Aunt Ottilie, hunting for an ashtray in which to flick the ash tip of her cigarette. "I thought you'd be out with your friends."

"Don't let us interrupt you, dear," Mrs. Banister said to Hilary. "Go on with your practicing. Hilary is preparing for her recital next month," she explained to Aunt Ottilie, who was peering hard at a small picture hanging over the couch. The picture, an etching, had hung in Mr. Banister's study. He had moved it to the living room, where everyone agreed it looked much better.

With a look of relief, Aunt Ottilie stepped back from the picture and sniffed. "For a moment, Lydia darling, I thought it was a *real* Picasso."

"It's a real *Braque*," said Mrs. Banister gazing fondly at the valuable etching, "although sometimes it's difficult to tell . . . especially if you don't know too much about art," she added sweetly.

Aunt Ottilie made a sour face.

Score one for Mom, Hilary thought. Oh, what she wouldn't have given at that moment to be able to play well—really fantastically well! If only she could plunge into some tremendous, majestic work and sweep Aunt Ottilie (and her precious Sally Anne) right smack out of the room, out of the house—O U T!

Instead, she plinked into the Mazurka.

Looking pleased with herself, Mrs. Banister fluffed the couch pillows, collected the dirty ashtray from beneath Aunt Ottilie's cigarette, and headed toward the door. "I think we should let Hilary go on with her practicing," she said to Aunt Ottilie. Hilary began playing very fast, trying to make it sound difficult and complicated. "Play with *expression*, dear," said Mrs. Banister as she left the room.

Wounded, Aunt Ottilie could draw blood. She gave Hilary a scorching smile and said, "Don't worry, Hilary dear, *I* never could learn to play, either." And with that she swept after her sister-in-law.

That did it! Krrrong-Krrreeeng! Krrrong-Krrreeeng! CRASH! Hilary brought her fists down on the piano and bounced them along the keyboard. A series of anguished, dissonant chords roared from the instrument.

"STOP THAT! Stop that this instant!" cried Mrs. Banister bursting into the room. "What on earth are you doing, Hilary? You're destroying the piano!"

"And my ears!" shrilled Aunt Ottilie, right behind her.

Good! More Krrrong-Krrreeeng! She hated the piano.

She hated music. She hated Aunt Ottilie's ears. She hated Everybody!

"Hilary, go to your room this minute," ordered her mother. "And stay there until you come to your senses. It's early to bed for you tonight, young lady. I'm afraid you're overtired."

"Overtired!" screamed Hilary, jumping up from the piano. "I'm not overtired. Every time you get mad at me, you say it's because I go to bed too late. I could go to bed at six o'clock. I could sleep a hundred million hours and it still wouldn't make any difference!" She stopped to breathe.

"There's no need to yell," shouted Mrs. Banister.

"I'm not yelling," shrieked Hilary, bringing her fists down on the keyboard. The piano screamed.

"My-oh-my, aren't we upset today," said Aunt Ottilie.

Mortified, Mrs. Banister shook an angry finger at Hilary. "At the rate you're going, young lady, you'll disgrace us all at the recital."

"Good. GOOD! I hope I do," screamed Hilary as she ran out of the room, almost knocking Aunt Ottilie over.

Aunt Ottilie brushed herself off. "Lydia darling, do forgive me if I run along now. Archer and I have a dinner appointment," she announced. "And anyway, I hate to be in the way during family squabbles."

Hilary dashed into her room, stumble-kicked her way through the pile of boxes on the floor, and flung herself across her bed. She lay there sobbing and yanking at her hair in helpless fury. She hated them all, but most of all she hated Hilary Banister.

A little later her father appeared at the door. "May I come in?"

No answer.

He sat down on the edge of her bed, started to put a hand on her shoulder, thought better of it, and dropped it back in his lap. He tried to comfort her. "According to your mother," he said, waving at the mess on the floor, "I ought to take out life insurance before coming in here." He laughed uncomfortably.

Hilary refused to answer. She refused to look up. She just held her breath and kept silent. Her father sat there a moment, awkwardly. Then with a sigh, he got up and went away. Glop ran from her nose. Her face felt red and hot. What had started it? She tried to remember. Then Aunt Ottilie's words rang through her head and the sobs started all over again.

Later that evening, Waldo poked his nose timidly into her room. She started to tell him to get out but changed her mind.

He stood at the edge of the pile of boxes and looked at her.

"What happened?"

Hilary shrugged.

"You flipped?"

"I guess so."

"Aunt Ottilie?"

"Umm."

"The recital?"

"Umm."

"Are they really going to make you play?"

"What do you care?" she cried, and started sobbing again.

"O.K., O.K. I'll let you borrow my new record if you like," he offered, trying to calm her down. Then he had an idea. "You know what you could do," he said. "You could practice real hard—say, two hours a day—and learn everything so well that nothing could go wrong." Immediately, Waldo knew he'd said the wrong thing.

Nobody spoke. A long shudder of breath racked Hilary's body. And another, shallower. The lump in her throat began to break up. She looked up at her brother. "You know what I wish?" she said finally. "I wish that for one hour I could be someone else."

"That's crazy," said Waldo. "Who'd you be?"

"The greatest pianist that ever lived. I'd show them . . ."

"That's stupid," said Waldo. "I'd be God. Then I could grant myself the power to be anybody I wanted to be, for as long as I wanted." He thought for a moment. "Why don't you get her to play it for you?"

"Get who?"

"Miss Orpheo. She could, you know. She . . ." Waldo broke off uncertainly. She could what?

But Hilary wasn't listening. She was thinking. If for one hour—even half an hour . . .

"Hilary! Your hands? What are you doing?"

Hilary was moving her fingers in the air, playing the piano.

"Wow, you've really flipped."

"Maybe," said Hilary. "And maybe not!"

8

What Hilary Heard

Three days later, after her piano lesson, Hilary sat curled in an armchair in the library of the Henrietta St. George Music School. She had started her homework while waiting for Cookie, whose lesson was longer.

The friendly library was the only part of the old mansion that had escaped renovation when the handsome building was converted into a charmless stack of music-lesson rooms and forced to earn its way as a music school. Nobody ever went to the library. But it was there. And you could go to it if you were waiting for someone and didn't know anyone in the school to talk to.

Shelves of books, in handsome leather bindings, lined the oak-paneled walls of the room. A few deep, plushy chairs still remained, instead of the hard benches and plastic-covered seats found everywhere else. And opposite Hilary there was a fireplace—never used now. Luckily, the cold fluorescent lamps, whose sickly green light had invaded the rest of the school, had not found their way to the library. Here, the original lamps in their worn, discolored shades cast pools of soft, golden light, filling the room with a glow. The library was a nice place—the only human thing in the whole school.

She concentrated on her math homework. "Find the union of set A and B, in which the elements . . ."

Gradually she became aware of voices: people talking, somewhere. She looked around, puzzled. She was alone. No . . . that wasn't it. The sounds seemed to be coming from the opposite wall. She hopped from her chair, stepped across to the fireplace, and listened again. How strange. The voices were coming from the conservatory, a small recital room adjoining the library. They had a hollow, metallic ring. The sound was probably being carried by a pipe in the wall, or something behind the fireplace. Hilary bent down. The voices grew louder. It was Madame St. George and . . . someone . . . Someone, nothing! It was Miss Orpheo. They seemed to be having an argument. Madame St. George's shrill voice kept getting higher and higher. Miss Orpheo's lower voice was less distinct.

"Madame," Hilary heard Miss Orpheo say, "do you really think I enjoy teaching pupils like . . . *mumble* . . . *mumble* . . ." Hilary pressed her ear against the wall, straining to hear. "Over and over again, week after week, I listen to the same mistakes, the same dreadful sounds . . . to watch a beautiful musical instrument . . . pounded to death."

Hilary almost fell into the fireplace.

"Well, really! Miss Orpheo." Madame St. George sounded shocked.

". . . and why?" continued Miss Orpheo's voice. ". . . because they don't practice, because they don't care, and because they have no . . . *mumble* . . . *mumble . . . buzzzzz . . .*"

Damn! Miss Orpheo had lowered her voice and Hilary couldn't hear what it was the pupils didn't have. How maddening!

Now Madame St. George was speaking again. "Really, Miss Orpheo," she cried, "I am appalled! If our students cause you such pain, I daresay you might prefer to teach somewhere else."

Miss Orpheo ignored this. She continued speaking in that tight, clipped voice Hilary knew so well. Hilary could imagine the expression on her face. "The parents provide a child," said Miss Orpheo, "they buy a piano, they buy music, they buy a piano teacher—and then they wash their hands of the whole affair. Once everything is paid for, they expect *me* to produce a miracle. Do they think I am a magician?"

Hilary gulped and turned red.

Madame St. George was saying something. " . . . all have parents to contend with . . . negative attitude . . . most unfortunate, indeed. My dear Miss Orpheo, I would have you know that the parents in this school are dedicated to music, and—if I may say so," she trilled, "devoted to *me.* They appreciate what we do for their children, and I am certain the children themselves agree."

"You wish it!" Hilary gasped.

"There are only three weeks left to the recital," Madame St. George continued. "How . . . er . . . is she doing?"

My God! Hilary's stomach froze. They were talking about her! She felt weak. She glanced nervously over her shoulder to make certain she was still alone. It would be hard to explain what she was doing crouching against the fireplace. Talking to the bricks, or something?

"Nonsense!" she heard Madame St. George say. "Everyone plays at our friendly little recitals . . ." (Hilary almost choked.) ". . . a Henrietta St. George tradition . . . and I might remind you, Miss Orpheo, part of our philosophy at this school—that the spirit of music is the Spirit of Giving."

"But in this particular case," protested Miss Orpheo, "it might not be wise. After all, she played last year."

"How well I remember!" said Madame St. George nastily.

"But perhaps if she had time to gain confidence . . ."

"*Assurdo!*" screamed Madame St. George. "Ridiculous! Playing for an audience is excellent discipline. She is a year older now. The experience will be good for her."

"But Madame, she is not only very nervous . . . *mumble . . . mumble . . .* not very well prepared."

The reply was lost. Both voices tuned out to an inaudible blur. They must have moved across the room.

Hilary squatted on the floor, numb, unable to believe her ears. "Wow!" she kept saying over and over to herself. "Oh wow!"

Now she could hear Madame St. George coming closer again. She pressed against the wall. "As I always say, Miss Orpheo," said Madame St. George, "'children *are* what they are made!' Perhaps you ought to consider whether, indeed, *you* are not to blame," she snapped. "Quite frankly, Miss Orpheo, if you do not approve of our methods, perhaps you might be wise to seek other employment . . . a place where your special understanding of children would be appreciated."

The old witch! Hilary clenched her fists.

"Oh, Madame," said Miss Orpheo hastily, "that is not what I meant." (Miss Orpheo sounded different, tired. "Don't give up!" Hilary wanted to shout to her.) "I was only suggesting . . ."

There was a pause, more mumbling, "We'll see about that," from Miss Orpheo. (About what? Hilary wondered.) And then something must have happened, because the clouds scattered. The storm was over. Madame St. George's voice turned sugary once again. She had won her point; the unpleasant matter was closed. "I am so pleased we understand each other, Miss Orpheo," she twittered. "After so many years in this school, I do not doubt you have come to understand the wisdom of our methods. I know that you will be sensible in the future, and that the Henrietta St. George Music School may expect the same excellent co-operation you have always given us."

Evidently the conversation was over, because a moment later Madame St. George came down the hall *clippity-clop*, past the library, *clippity-clop-clop*, fading away as she marched upstairs, probably to her office.

Hilary scrambled to her feet and jumped back into her chair. She sat there, upright and rigid, burning with anger and embarrassment. It just didn't seem possible, but Miss Orpheo had actually stood up for her. She couldn't believe it. And now, in about three weeks she was going to have to go out on that stage—and die. Hilary swallowed hard, feeling the muscles in her throat tighten. They both would be disgraced, and Miss Orpheo would probably be fired.

She felt sorry for Miss Orpheo, in a way. It must be horrible to spend your life giving piano lessons to children who hadn't an ounce of talent, who only played because their parents made them. If Miss Orpheo quit or lost her job, there was probably nothing else she could do to earn her living. She didn't have a husband to support her. She'd probably starve to death. Hilary sighed, struggling with her feelings. She could almost hear her mother's words: "Now Hilary, be kind. After all, Miss Orpheo's had a difficult life." It would be easier to feel sorry for Miss Orpheo, Hilary thought, if she weren't so busy feeling sorry for herself. She knew all about Miss Orpheo's "difficult life" from her mother. In her head, Hilary called it: *Miss Orpheo's Story*.

When she was a young girl (if you could imagine Miss Orpheo being young), Priscilla Orpheo had been a pupil of a pupil of a pupil of the great Franz Liszt. Liszt's teacher had been Czerny (who wrote all the exercises), and Czerny's teacher had been Beethoven. In some way, Hilary gathered, the spirit of Beethoven, admittedly a little thin, was presumed to hover over her lessons.

Alexander Orpheo, Miss Orpheo's father, had been a brilliant violinist. Tall, aristocratic, and handsome, he had toured all the great concert stages of Europe and America, thrilling audiences with his dazzling technique and his great musical artistry. He could play so fast that sparks seemed to fly from his violin bow. At other times, the violinist's beautiful soaring tone went straight to the hearts of all who heard him, leaving eyes bright and moist. According to Hilary's mother, who had heard it from Martha Claxton, Alexander Orpheo was also conceited and selfish. Next to music, his greatest love was himself.

His wife and daughter also adored him, and by the time Miss Orpheo was twelve years old, she began to act as her father's accompanist. In addition to her own musical studies, she spent many hours each day helping her beloved but demanding father prepare his concert repertoire. A handsome young man—who later became famous himself—served as her father's official accompanist for actual concert engagements. If her father played a violin concerto, a great symphony orchestra replaced the piano transcription provided by Miss Orpheo during their practice hours. For years, Priscilla Orpheo's home was a hotel room containing a piano and three violins. It could be in any city.

Miss Orpheo was seventeen when her mother died. After that, she gradually assumed other duties. She dealt with managers and piano tuners, supervised concert arrangements, attended to travel reservations, paid bills, and wrote letters. Lastly, she saw to it that her father's concert attire was always fresh and ready and that the diamond shirt studs (a gift of the French Government) sparkled in the little velvet box on his dressing table. Miss Orpheo never appeared on stage, except once, to turn pages for the obnoxious pianist who kept his nose up in the air and never bothered to say thank you. If she ever regretted the loss of her own promising career, the young girl said nothing.

Indeed, everyone thought it wonderful that the great violinist had such a devoted daughter. How satisfying it must be for her, they said. What an inspiring experience. There were a few—but very few—who disagreed. It was a downright shame, they snorted, the way the young girl was exploited by her father and permitted to sacrifice her career. Those few who had overheard Miss Orpheo practicing in the studio were surprised. She played like an angel! Even her father agreed—after all, she was *his* daughter—but he insisted that the concert stage was no place for a "lady." When you came down to it, people had to admit, Priscilla Orpheo was plain, very plain, indeed. No . . . after all . . . she was probably not suited to a career on the concert stage. Too modest and retiring. The girl lacked temperament; she lacked fire. They shook their heads. What a pity, they said, and went away.

Priscilla Orpheo seemed to agree. Eventually she abandoned her own studies in order to accompany her father on a concert tour of Europe: London, Paris, Vienna, Berlin, Prague, Stockholm, Rome . . . Alexander Orpheo's performances were strung about the Continent like beads on a necklace. However, one evening in Budapest it came to an end. While playing the Brahms Violin Concerto, he suffered a heart attack and died. Miss Orpheo brought her father home, had him buried next to her mother, and sold his priceless Stradivarius violin to pay the bills.

Time passed. No one knew what she did or how she lived in the intervening years. She was said to be living in Europe, in South America, in the Far East—flitting here and there, as if running from her life. Then one day Miss Orpheo appeared in New York City, complete with ragpicker dresses and rummage-sale shoes. She became a member of the Henrietta St. George Music School, assigned, Hilary was convinced, to teaching the least promising students. Miss Orpheo was dedicated to her work and rarely referred to the past. Once in a while somebody would say, "Priscilla Orpheo? Wasn't she the daughter of Alexander Orpheo?" After a while they stopped saying even that.

A hand gripped Hilary's shoulder from behind. "Hilary Banister! Are you mental . . . or something? Staring into space like that?"

Startled, Hilary spun around and looked up. It was Cookie. "Cookie, I've got the wildest thing to tell you. You'll never believe it."

Cookie put her violin case down. "I know—they're not going to make you play."

Hilary gave her a look. Then she told Cookie about the argument.

"Wow! You mean, through *there?*" Cookie stooped to

examine the fireplace. "You're really trapped now. They'll fire her if you don't play, don't you think?"

No answer.

Cookie raised her voice slightly. "I said, Hil, it looks like you're trapped. I don't envy you."

Still no answer. Hilary was staring at the fireplace. She listened. Not voices this time. Something else . . .

Cookie gave her a poke. "Hilary! Have you gone deaf? What's the matter with you?"

"Shh!" Hilary put her finger to her lips and moved toward the fireplace. "C'mere. Listen."

In the next room someone was playing the piano. The notes rose and fell in a broad, rippling pattern from which emerged the most beautiful melody Hilary had ever heard. Whoever was playing seemed to have become part of the instrument, simply willing the music, so that the fingers drifting over the keys seemed unnecessary. The piano pleaded and sang, responding joyfully to the person in command. The melody surged with the swell of notes and then died away. The mood darkened. Storms of chords in an unhappy minor key raged across the keyboard, rolling upward in an angry crescendo. Just as the piano seemed about to explode, the reckless chords began to collect themselves, drifting in groups, becoming orderly and once more under control. And then, when the moment was right, the troubled minor key dissolved. Like sunlight breaking from behind the clouds, the beautiful theme returned—shimmering, dreamlike, and lovelier than ever.

"Shh!" Hilary motioned Cookie to follow. They tiptoed into the hall. The door to the conservatory was open. They approached cautiously. Abruptly, the music stopped. They peeked in, but it was too late. The room was empty.

Hastily, the girls withdrew to the library. Footsteps sounded in the hall outside. Someone passed the library door, moved quietly down the hall, and disappeared.

"Her?" Cookie asked, wide-eyed.

"I don't know," replied Hilary. "You saw. There was no one there." She thought for a moment. "You know, I've never really heard her play—except my dumb little pieces."

Cookie shook her head, disapprovingly. "I couldn't stand it if they didn't play for you," she said. "If they didn't play, how could you tell if they knew how?"

Hilary smiled. It was true. She knew that Miss Orpheo could play, but from the little she had heard at her lessons, she never dreamed it would be like this. Miss Orpheo's kind of music would be tidy and tight—typewriter music, with the dry, mechanical sound of pecking keys. The stormy, romantic music they had just heard, with the beautiful singing theme that made you want to cry, did not seem to be the kind of music you'd expect from an old-maid piano teacher in ragpicker dresses.

"C'mon, Hilary, it's late," Cookie reminded her. "Let's go."

Hilary stood as if in a trance.

"Hilary! Snap out of it," Cookie ordered. "We've got tons of homework."

"Yeah, I know." Hilary buttoned her coat and pulled her long hair free of the collar.

"If she's so good," said Cookie as they hurried down the stairs, "why doesn't *she* play your recital?"

"Oh sure," said Hilary laughing. "We look a lot alike."

Together, the girls stepped out into the street. It was after five and almost dark. In November, when the sun was busy in other parts of the world, evening arrived long before it was wanted. Wrapping their arms around their books to keep warm, the girls hurried home. Taxis honked, lights blinked on, the wind nipped. People strained upward from the depths of the subway, pushing out into the busy streets. Others jammed into the crowded buses, groaning and snorting through the city traffic. People everywhere—the way people do in New York—were hurrying home. Some had no homes to go to. But for a while, before they drifted away, they mingled in the great stream of those who had a place to go when the city grew dark and cold. A night like this, Hilary thought, made you especially grateful for the cheerful lights and friendly warmth of your own home, a place that belonged to you and where you belonged.

"I'll speak to you after dinner," said Cookie as they parted.

"Don't forget," Hilary called after her. She turned in to her house.

Mike, the doorman, pulled open the heavy door for her. "Well, I guess winter'll be here soon," he said.

"Mmm." Hilary stepped into the warm lobby. She wondered where Miss Orpheo was now. Inside, somewhere, she hoped.

9

Mr. Ferdinand Comes... and Goes

Several days later, Hilary and Waldo came home from school and found their mother waiting for them in the kitchen.

"Children, Mr. Ferdinand, the piano tuner, is coming today—at four o'clock. I want you to be very good. Absolutely no noise."

"Why?" they both asked at once.

"Because Mr. Ferdinand is a very fine piano tuner."

"If he's so good, then noise shouldn't bother him." Waldo grabbed a handful of cookies to go with the milk his mother had set out for him.

"He's temperamental," Mrs. Banister explained. "I've been trying to get an appointment with him for months. According to Martha Claxton . . ."

97

"Yuch! I hate her," said Hilary.

"She has that dumb son with the peanut head," Waldo added.

"Children!" said Mrs. Banister. "You mustn't hate. And Freddy Claxton can't help the shape of his head. Besides, he's not dumb; he can talk."

"He's stuck-up," said Hilary.

"As I was saying," Mrs. Banister raised her voice slightly, "according to Martha Claxton, Mr. Ferdinand will not tune your piano if he doesn't like the piano. And he won't tune your piano if he doesn't like *you*." She looked hard at Waldo.

"Who needs him!" muttered Waldo.

"*We* do," said Mrs. Banister. "It's an honor. Mr. Ferdinand tunes pianos for great musicians like Rubinstein and Heifetz."

"Heifetz plays the violin," said Hilary, popping a cookie into her mouth.

"He must have a piano, too," replied Mrs. Banister, annoyed.

Waldo put a straw into his milk and began blowing bubbles.

"WALDO!" cried Mrs. Banister. "Stop that! Stop that this minute!"

Hilary made a face and rolled her eyes. "How can you be such a pig, Waldo?"

"Practice," said Waldo grinning. "Why does the piano have to be tuned?" he demanded of his mother.

"Because it's out of tune," replied Mrs. Banister.

"How do you know? It sounds O.K. to me," said Waldo. Waldo wasn't interested in facts. If you said it was raining, Walso would say it wasn't; if you said it was *not* raining, Waldo would say it was.

"The piano ought to be out of tune. It hasn't been tuned in ages," insisted Mrs. Banister, who had no idea whether it was out of tune or not.

"Well, if it's out of tune and nobody can tell, why do you have to have it tuned?" asked Waldo triumphantly.

"Because we're having a dinner party tomorrow," explained Mrs. Banister, "and someone may want to play the piano."

Waldo's answer was to blow more bubbles. Then he got the giggles and the milk went spraying into Hilary's eyes.

"Waldo!" Hilary cried, jumping out of her seat.

Mrs. Banister began screaming at Waldo.

"Honestly, Mom," Hilary complained, "he's the most revolting kid I ever saw. Why did you have to have *him* for a child?"

"Someday," said Mrs. Banister darkly, addressing both of them, "you'll have children of your own. Then you'll see what it's like."

"Hey? What did I do?" protested Hilary.

But Mrs. Banister turned and stalked out of the kitchen.

At four o'clock the doorbell rang. Mrs. Banister paused to smooth her hair, then opened the door. In walked Mr. Ferdinand.

"My God!" whispered Hilary.

"He's about two feet tall," said Waldo. The children were hiding behind the living-room door.

"Not really," said Hilary, "but he's shorter than Mom. It's his head. It's too big for his body."

"What's so special about him? The way Mom acts, you'd think it was the King of England or something."

"Shhh . . . I can't hear."

"How nice to see you, Mr. Ferdinand," said Mrs. Banister. "We're so pleased you could find time. Mrs. Claxton spoke so very highly of you." Hilary recognized the little trilling voice her mother used when she wanted to impress people.

"Hmmf," sniffed Mr. Ferdinand, "all my clients do. I just finished tuning fifteen pianos for the new Music Center."

"How marvelous," said Mrs. Banister.

"Not marvelous," said Mr. Ferdinand. "Terrible! The pianos they make today are abominable. Is there someplace I may leave my hat and coat?"

"Why certainly," replied Mrs. Banister, hurrying to take his things. "What a pity. Fifteen pianos, you say."

"Not a pity. Serves them right for not listening to me. I warned them not to buy those pianos."

"Oh, I do hope you will like our piano," said Mrs. Banister, nervously. "It's a very fine Steinway, you know."

"My dear Mrs. Banister," said Mr. Ferdinand, drawing himself up to his full height and pinning her with his eyes, "there are Steinways—and there are *Steinways!*" His voice rose to a shrill pitch.

"The piano is . . . this way," said Mrs. Banister, showing the piano tuner into the living room.

"I can see that for myself," said Mr. Ferdinand irrita-

bly. He carried a black leather bag containing his piano-
tuning instruments. "If you will be so good, Mrs. Banister, please stand back from the piano.

Mrs. Banister obeyed hastily.

"Wow!" said Waldo. "What a pill."

"Shh," Hilary cautioned. She felt sorry for her
mother. For a little man, Mr. Ferdinand certainly was
obnoxious. The children stood behind the door waiting
to see what the piano tuner would do next.

First, he lifted the lid of the piano, supporting it with
the wooden prop. With distaste he examined the ring
mark where the vase of flowers usually stood. Then
stretching on tiptoe, he ran his finger inside along the
dampers, the felt-covered blocks on top of the strings.
"Dirt!" he announced, pointing his blackened finger at
Mrs. Banister. She flushed, clasped her hands and un-
clasped them.

Now Mr. Ferdinand moved around to the keyboard
and, still standing, struck several chords.

Mrs. Banister waited uneasily. "I'm afraid it's out of
tune," she said, breaking the uncomfortable silence.

"It is." The piano tuner continued his investigation
for a few more minutes while Mrs. Banister hovered, not
daring to come too close.

Finally, Mr. Ferdinand looked up and delivered his
verdict. "In case you are not aware of it, you have a very
fine instrument here."

"So we've been told," said Mrs. Banister smiling with
relief.

". . . but badly neglected," he continued.

The children began to inch in front of the door.

"Nevertheless," continued Mr. Ferdinand, "I will tune your piano." He patted the instrument affectionately. The piano, at least, had passed the test; they were going to be friends. "One thing more," said Mr. Ferdinand sternly. "I do not wish to be disturbed while I work." He glanced in the direction of the living-room door. Hilary yanked Waldo back behind the door.

"Don't worry, Mr. Ferdinand," said Mrs. Banister, "no one will disturb you. I'll be in the kitchen. Should there be anything you need, just call."

"There won't be," said Mr. Ferdinand with a snort, and opening his black bag he set to work.

Mrs. Banister tiptoed out of the room, delighted to leave the difficult little man to himself.

The children watched, fascinated. Mr. Ferdinand seated himself, loosened some screws along the front of the piano, and unexpectedly, pulled out the entire keyboard, resting it across his knees. So that's what it looked like inside. It was really wild! The piano tuner had exposed the *action*—the felt-covered wooden hammers and dampers that were connected to the ivory keys, and which, ordinarily, were hidden from view. Resting on Mr. Ferdinand's lap, the keyboard looked like a giant set of false teeth, hanging perilously from the piano's jaws.

Shaking his head and mumbling to himself, the piano tuner leaned forward to examine the padded mallets. After a while, he stood up. "There you are, my beauty," he said, and with a shove, he pushed the action back into place. The funny-looking hammers and dampers disappeared. Having swallowed its working parts, the sleek piano was again a dignified study in black and white.

Next, Mr. Ferdinand reached into his black bag, pulled out a tuning fork and struck it. Then, string by string, tenderly and patiently, he twisted the metal tuning pins, bringing each string to its proper pitch.

Ping-peeng; Da, da-dum; da-da-DUM . . . The tuning made a strange, forward-backward marching dance as the piano moved up the scale with Mr. Ferdinand. Suddenly, *prrrronk!* The piano gave a strangled yelp. Mr. Ferdinand frowned and reached into the broad belly of the piano. Muttering to himself, he pulled something out of the piano and put it in his pocket. Hilary couldn't see what it was.

"My poor beauty," said Mr. Ferdinand to the piano, "what you have to put up with, eh? Children with their dirty, sticky hands banging out their horrible little pieces."

Ping-peennng; Da, da-da-DUM, went the piano as if in response.

"Oh-ho? What have we here?" Mr. Ferdinand bent his nose to the keyboard and ran his fingers over one of the keys. He shook his head in disgust. "They take pencils—ha!—and Rrrrrrrrp up and down your white keys. Barbarians!"

Hilary poked Waldo in the ribs. "Quit it," he whispered, poking her back.

"They give parties," continued Mr. Ferdinand. "People set drinks down on you. They ruin your beautiful finish." He removed something from the piano and put it in his pocket. "They spill ashes into . . ."

Peeng-PEEEEEENG! whined the piano.

"and hot coffee . . ."

PEEEEEEEEENNNG!

"And they sit on you!" Before the piano could comment, Mr. Ferdinand rattled off a series of chords. "Ah, good," he said, rubbing his hands. He seemed pleased. Gradually, the piano was responding to his patience and skill. "Don't worry, my friend," he said, "I am here to help you."

Pulling a big messy handkerchief from his pocket, Mr. Ferdinand mopped his brow, and then went back to work. But he had stopped talking. Hilary and Waldo got tired of watching and went into the kitchen to talk to their mother.

"Stevie's father has something better than a dumb piano," Waldo announced. "A stereo he built himself. It plays loud, too. Really loud."

Mrs. Banister shook her head. "Loud noise gives me a terrible headache."

"Not me," said Hilary.

"Not me," said Waldo. "The louder the better."

"If you children go on playing that ghastly stuff," said Mrs. Banister with a shudder, "you'll all be deaf by the time you grow up."

"Why, Mom!" Waldo protested. "The music's great!" He began playing an imaginary set of drums.

"Really, Mom," Hilary urged, "you should listen sometime."

"I do not consider *that* music," said Mrs. Banister. "Besides, it hurts my ears."

"*Your* music hurts *our* ears," said Hilary.

"Classical music, yuch!" Waldo made a face.

Hilary shook her head. How anybody could stand listening to those screeching opera singers her mother loved so much was beyond her. Frankly, their music gave *her* a headache.

Inside, Mr. Ferdinand had stopped the ping-peenging. Now he began to play long, rolling arpeggios, gamboling up the keyboard from the deep roar of the base to the tinkle of the highest treble.

"Why doesn't he play something real?" Hilary asked her mother.

"They rarely do," said Mrs. Banister, smiling. "I only hope he's willing to come back again."

Just then, Mr. Ferdinand called. "Mrs. Banister, may I see you please."

"I'm coming," she answered as she hurried into the room. This time Hilary and Waldo followed, standing timidly behind their mother.

"I have done my best, madam," said Mr. Ferdinand, blotting his face with the enormous handkerchief. "A piano that stands so close to the window and the steam heat . . . bah! What can you expect?" He wiped his face again and began packing his tools. "You should move your piano," he announced.

Where would they put it? Hilary wondered. She couldn't imagine her father disturbing the "rhythm" of the living room, just to protect the piano from the steam heat. Everything in the Banister home, from the furniture to the ashtrays, had been selected and placed to create what her father called "a lyrical interplay of forms"—whatever that was. Even the pictures were hung in keeping with a "geometry of color," which only Hilary's father (and a few special people) could see. Obviously, the piano would have to live with the steam.

"Maybe we could leave the heat off," Mrs. Banister offered softly.

Mr. Ferdinand shrugged. He snapped his bag shut and looked up. "Some pianos are wild, you know. This one is." But he smiled when he spoke, and for the second time he patted the instrument fondly. Perhaps because he liked their piano, Hilary thought, the piano tuner seemed a little friendlier.

"I shall return in three months to tune it again," said Mr. Ferdinand. "Would you like to try it?"

"Oh dear, no," said Mrs. Banister, shrinking back. "I don't play." With a wave of her hand, she indicated Hilary. "My daughter is the musician in the family," she said proudly. "Hilary is a student at the Henrietta St. George Music School."

Hilary winced. Mr. Ferdinand gave her a sharp look. Hilary could tell he wasn't impressed by eleven-year-old "musicians." She didn't blame him.

"This is my son, Waldo," said Mrs. Banister, reaching behind herself and pulling Waldo forward. "Waldo will start piano next year."

Waldo glared at his mother. His ears looked pointier —the way they always did when he was angry. But he nodded politely to Mr. Ferdinand, who ignored him.

They waited for Hilary to try the piano.

Hilary was embarrassed. How could she play her dumb little pieces after listening to the confident, thundering sounds the piano tuner had made. And he hadn't even been playing! "I don't know anything," she mumbled.

"Play that pretty little piece with the trills—the one I like so much," suggested Mrs. Banister.

"I don't have that any more," said Hilary, avoiding Mr. Ferdinand's eyes.

"Play anything, dear," said Mrs. Banister hopefully.

O.K., she would. Hilary stood at the piano and struck middle C, then D, E, F; she played G and stopped. Mr. Ferdinand wasn't listening. Obviously, he didn't need *her* to test the piano.

Mr. Ferdinand addressed Hilary's mother. "Mrs. Claxton led me to believe that this piano was used for chamber music. Consequently, I have raised the pitch somewhat. Most of my clients prefer it that way."

It was Mrs. Banister's turn to be embarrassed. She had no idea what Mr. Ferdinand was talking about.

"You see, madam," continued Mr. Ferdinand sharply, "I was under the impression this was a musical family."

The top of the piano was still open. While Mr. Ferdinand explained how much he charged for his work, Hilary and Waldo peeked into the piano. A stout web of overlapping strings fanned out across the soundboard, running from the turning pins to the iron frame on the outside.

"It looks just like a harp lying on its side," Hilary whispered.

Waldo couldn't resist. He ran a pencil across the strings. Brrrrrrrrrrring! Mr. Ferdinand wheeled about. "Little boy, don't do that!" he snapped. Waldo cringed.

"Those strings produce nearly eighteen tons of tension on the piano frame. If a string should break . . ."

"Wow!" Waldo's eyes were wide.

"How remarkable!" said Mrs. Banister.

"A grand piano," lectured Mr. Ferdinand, "has at least twelve thousand parts and takes about a year to build. And you, little boy, with your stupid pencil," he said glaring at Waldo, "how long will you take to destroy it? Eh?"

Waldo retreated to his mother, who put her arm around him protectively.

Mr. Ferdinand noticed that Hilary was still looking at the inside of the piano. "That is the soundboard in there, beneath the strings—the soul of the instrument! And in front here, inside and underneath," he pointed, "the *action*. You know, of course, how it works?"

Hilary shook her head. She did not know "of course." The inside of the piano was so different from the outside. Closed, standing there with its polished ebony finish and its gleaming ivory keys, haughty in its formal attire, the piano was ready for the most elegant concert stage. Inside was another matter. The spindly wooden hammers looked like a dizzy assembly line in a crazy old-fashioned factory.

"In here, below the strings," explained Mr. Ferdinand, warming to the subject he loved, "there are eighty-eight wooden hammers covered with felt. One for each key. The key is only a lever. When you press the key, the hammer is thrown up against the strings, causing them to vibrate. It strikes," he said dramatically, "and falls back—even if you still hold the key down. Watch!" He demonstrated.

So that's how it worked. Hilary was surprised. The hammers were *underneath* the strings. They struck *up*. Then what were those clumpy-looking wooden blocks that sat on top of the strings? she wondered.

"These are the dampers," said Mr. Ferdinand. "When you strike the key—so!—you lift the damper. The strings vibrate. When you release the key—so!—the damper falls back on the strings and stops the sound. It is beautiful, ah!"

Hilary nodded. It was neat, all right. You strike the key, which throws the hammer and lifts the damper. The real playing went on inside the piano, sort of by remote control. In a rapid passage of music, she could just see the blizzard of flinging hammers and hop-popping dampers.

"Mom, can't we leave the top of the piano open?" asked Waldo, breaking into Hilary's thoughts. "It looks better that way . . . like it's flying."

"No, we can't leave it open," replied Mrs. Banister. She explained that in a city apartment it was quite unnecessary. Too loud.

"Stevie's parents leave it up," objected Waldo.

"That's because they don't know any better," explained his mother. "A city apartment is not a concert hall."

For once, Mr. Ferdinand looked grateful.

With its great lid floating above it, the piano looked very romantic. Yet, Hilary had to agree with her mother. "Lifting the lid is showing off, dope," she told Waldo.

"And besides, dirt gets in," said Mrs. Banister.

"Speaking of dirt," said Mr. Ferdinand unpleasantly, "I have removed a few . . . er . . . things from inside the *action!*" Mr. Ferdinand spoke as if to say that this was exactly what you would expect from a family that had an eleven-year-old child who played the C-major scale, and another child who stuck pencils into the piano; a family that refused to throw out the living-room furniture in order to protect the piano from the steam heat. While he talked, Mr. Ferdinand reached into his pockets with both hands.

Mrs. Banister gasped.

Hilary couldn't believe her eyes. "My library card!"

"My water pistol," cried Waldo, snatching it and squirting it into the air. "Hey, real water!" Just in time, Mrs. Banister snatched the water pistol from Waldo.

The piano tuner continued emptying his pockets, dumping a strange assortment of objects on the table in front of them. In addition to the water pistol and library card, there were:

a marble
a jack
three paper clips
candy wrappers
a Chiclet
two pencils, a rubber band
hairpins
a subway token, a bubble gum comic
cigarette butts
half a Ritz cracker

the friendship ring Hilary had accused Waldo of taking
the bicycle lock Waldo had accused Hilary of stealing
a peach pit
a dried-out chicken bone
and
a
scrap of brown fabric

Waldo's eyes narrowed. He stared at the last item. For a moment, he thought it was . . . Then he dismissed the thought.

"If you don't mind my observing," said Mr. Ferdinand dryly, "a grand piano is a sensitive, delicate instrument—a work of art. It is not a storehouse," he hissed, "nor is it a restaurant." He pointed with distaste to the chicken bone and the peach pit.

Mrs. Banister gave a nervous laugh. "Oh dear, one would think someone had set up housekeeping in there," she said, trying to make a joke of the whole thing.

"One would, indeed."

"You know how children are," continued Mrs. Banister, smiling sweetly at Hilary and Waldo.

"Only too well," said Mr. Ferdinand, "which is why I don't have any! And now, good day to you, madam. I am already late for my next client, Anton Decibel—the composer, you know . . ." With that, he took his bag, his hat and coat, and departed.

No one was sorry.

10

The Vehicle of Art

"How come it's up?" asked Waldo, running his pocket comb across the piano strings. They had just finished the Piano-lesson Spell.

"Quit it, Waldo," said Hilary. "They're having a dinner party tonight. It's supposed to get dusted, or vacuumed . . . or something. Mr. Ferdinand said to."

"Why do they need a dinner party?" Waldo asked. "Who's coming?"

"Who knows? Who cares?" said Hilary, answering both questions. She brushed the rug lint from her sweater and made a face. "Aunt Ottilie and Uncle Archer, of course. Madame Kunigunde. The Claxtons—they always have them."

"At least there'll be FOOD," said Waldo.

"You hope."

"I KNOW. Mrs. Caraway's in the kitchen making those little hot-dog things, and the bakery just sent cake and cookies." Waldo gave the piano strings a final breep with his comb and bounced out of the room.

"They're not for you," Hilary yelled after him, and dashed into the kitchen to see if Mrs. Caraway would let her have a taste of something. Maybe there would be chocolate eclairs.

When Miss Orpheo arrived a few minutes later, she looked at the raised piano lid and frowned.

"My mother is having it cleaned," Hilary explained. "The piano tuner said we should."

Miss Orpheo pursed her lips. She gazed at the piano and for a fleeting moment a look of tender concern illumined her colorless face. It reminded Hilary of the way Mr. Ferdinand had looked at the piano.

"Well now, Hilary, shall we begin?" said Miss Orpheo finally. She took her seat next to the piano. She was wearing a mouse-gray ragpicker dress, trimmed with wilted lace. Hilary glanced sideways, squinting at her teacher. She tried to merge the image of paper-dry Miss Orpheo in her skinny ragpicker dress with the marvelous pianist she had heard playing in the music school conservatory. It was weird. It just didn't seem possible. Who are you, Miss Orpheo? Who *are* you?"

"Very well, thank you," replied Miss Orpheo. "How nice of you to ask."

Startled, Hilary blushed, and busied herself turning the pages of her music.

"Hilary!" Miss Orpheo turned to Hilary and looked at her. Whatever was left of young Priscilla Orpheo, Hilary thought, scanning Miss Orpheo's face for clues, it lay hidden behind the teacher's eyes. But the windows were locked and the key turned from inside.

Miss Orpheo was speaking. "I think that today we should begin with the Loosening-up Exercises. Perhaps if you are loose and relaxed *before* we begin, you will play . . . er . . ." (She didn't say "better," but Hilary knew that's what she meant) ". . . with more confidence." With that, she clattered to her feet and stepped to the center of the room. Apparently, Miss Orpheo was not ready to bring up the subject of the recital—not yet, anyway. Hilary was glad.

Together, they began the stretching exercises. *Up* to the ceiling, *down* to the floor. Hilary felt queer. Maybe it was the blood draining into her head as she hung over her toes. On and off, for a week, an idea had been floating around in her mind. It wasn't a real idea—just a twitch of feeling, indistinct, but promising, like one of her father's color slides when the projector was out of focus. Yesterday, after Mr. Ferdinand had left, the idea drifted into view again. Now, as she hung upside down over her toes, it reappeared, wheeling in front of her, teasing, inviting her to follow. "*Sometimes the craziest ideas . . .*" It grew stronger, sharper, spreading out into her fingertips, making them tingle and dance. "*I wish that for one hour . . . even for half an hour . . .*" Her own words went through her head. She shivered and stood up straight. The feeling was gone.

The Loosening-up Exercises moved into the more active phase: the part where they flew around the room bending and stretching and shaking their arms.

Play the Bach, Dear!

"Up-down, UP-DOWN. Little fingers loose," chanted Miss Orpheo.

They careened around the room. As they passed the piano, Miss Orpheo slowed down momentarily, and Hilary, struggling to capture the elusive idea before it vanished altogether, almost crashed into her. "Oh! I'm sorry!" she blurted out. Miss Orpheo nodded. Regaining her balance, the piano teacher flung herself into another circuit of the room, going faster and faster . . . Up-down, bend and stretch . . .

"*Why doesn't she play your recital?*" she heard Cookie say. "*The key is only a lever . . . the hammer is thrown up against the strings.*" And then, as they passed the piano, the parts of the idea, floating just out of reach in Hilary's head, suddenly came rushing together like the pieces of a jigsaw puzzle. "A *piano is not a storehouse* . . ." It was coming in now, bright and clear . . . "*Looks like someone has set up housekeeping . . .*" And there it was: not a thought, not a plan, but a nameless, wordless perception blazing in Hilary's head, casting everything else into shadow.

They were going faster now, almost flying. Hilary reached out toward the center of Miss Orpheo's back. Her fingers hovered there, just over the spot between the shoulder blades. She hesitated and tried to pull her hand back, but it resisted. It seemed drawn to Miss Orpheo's dress. A little flick? A little push . . . The gray speckles on the ragpicker dress wheeled and whirled, growing larger and larger, growing spotty and dotty, laughing and dancing into Hilary's eyes . . . Quick! Her hand touched. A gentle little tap and . . . Flip!

SHE DID IT!

Up, UP into the air; then down . . . DOWN, feet first into the piano flew Miss Orpheo, her long, skinny arms still stretched high above her head. As she went in, Hilary saw her reach out, knock loose the prop that held the lid, and lower the top of the piano case over her head. In a matter of seconds, the piano was closed and Miss Orpheo had disappeared inside.

"Hey, Hilary!" Waldo rushed from behind the living-room door, nodding his head vigorously. "Remember the time I was sick . . ."

"Shh!" Hilary clapped her hand over his mouth. They approached the piano and peeked into the opening behind the music rack. Now that it had happened, Hilary wasn't certain *what* had happened. Had she pushed Miss Orpheo? she wondered. Or had Orpheo gone in by herself? Certainly, Miss Orpheo seemed to know what was expected of her. Waldo was digging Hilary in the ribs trying to tell her something. She wished he would leave her alone.

She called into the piano. "Miss Orpheo? Miss Orpheo, are you there? Are you all right? We can't see you."

"Of course you can't," came Miss Orpheo's voice. It sounded far away. "I'm down here, in the *action*, beneath the hammers. Goodness, it's dusty." Miss Orpheo sneezed, setting the piano strings jangling.

"God bless you," said Hilary.

"Quick, Hilary, be good enough to get me a dust-cloth."

"Quick, Waldo," said Hilary, "run in the kitchen and bring an old dustcloth."

Play the Bach, Dear!

Waldo started to grumble. "Hurry!" Hilary commanded. Waldo tore off and came right back with a cookie he had filched and a new white dishtowel. Hilary scowled (they'd catch it from Mrs. Caraway) and snatched the towel from him.

"Over here, Hilary—behind the music rack," called Miss Orpheo's voice. "Just drop it down." Breep! Breeeeeep! The strings sounded in surprise as Miss Orpheo bustled around tidying up the inside of the piano. Suddenly, the top lifted slightly and the dirty, black dishtowel flew out of the piano and fell to the floor. Hilary bent to pick it up. "There," said Miss Orpheo. "The last time I wanted to do that I was interrupted."

Waldo turned red.

A note sounded. Then another note, and another . . . A scale. "Hilary!" From inside the piano Miss Orpheo's voice had an eerie, muffled quality. "Play your Bach Invention, please. And count!" Miss Orpheo began to sing in her high opera-singer voice: La-di da-di-DA, la-dee, DA-DEE. "Waldo," she called, "since you seem to have developed a new interest in music, you may stay and listen. Be so kind as to remove your arms from the top of the piano. The piano is the instrument of Mozart and Beethoven, Chopin and Schumann . . ." Her voice rose, trembling slightly. "The piano is a vehicle of art," she informed him, "NOT a public resting place."

Waldo jumped back with a start. "Yes'm," he gasped.

"Hilary, I am still waiting. Please begin," said Miss Orpheo.

Hilary sat down and began to play, scrambling to catch up to Miss Orpheo, who had started without her.

La-di da-di-DA . . . Hilary's hands were shaking. She glanced ahead at the music. The Horrible Spot was coming. She could never get through it without messing up. La-di da-di-DA . . . The notes were running downhill . . . two measures, one measure, one note—and out onto thin ice.

Miraculously, she found herself on the far side of the dangerous measure. She couldn't believe she'd made it. There was no time to think. Miss Orpheo pressed forward, pulling Hilary along with her. Together, they played into the second page. Hilary relaxed and her fingers began to unknot. Once, she glanced at Waldo. He was sitting on his hands on the couch staring at her. She smiled faintly at him. She knew what he was thinking. It didn't sound like Hilary playing. Well, actually it wasn't.

The music Hilary (rather, the piano) produced was unlike anything Hilary had ever heard herself play. Her fingers flew over the keyboard, swift and assured; the staccatos were bright and sharp, the rhythm steady and the accents—no longer accidents—were where they belonged. It wasn't surprising, of course, with Miss Orpheo inside the piano, working the hammers, lifting the dampers, supplying difficult notes, fending off wrong ones, always holding Hilary to a steady rhythm. *This is the way it goes . . . one-and, 2-and . . .* The Bach Invention sparkled, its crystal notes rising and falling like a fountain of water. For the first time, the piece made sense to Hilary.

"You play the right hand; I'll play the left," ordered Miss Orpheo as they began the Chopin Mazurka. Her voice came from deep down within the piano, somewhere below the bass strings. The Mazurka danced. It sounded lovely. At one point, Miss Orpheo scolded: "Hilary, please, you are drowning the music in pedal. As far as the pedal is concerned, you realize I must depend on you for that. I can do so much, and only so much," she said with a sniff.

After the Mazurka, they played Hilary's other pieces, and all the time Miss Orpheo was there inside the piano, filling in, patching up, shaping and phrasing the music. Hilary concentrated on the pedal. Her jitters disappeared. It was fun to play with Miss Orpheo as a partner, she decided. For the first time in her life, Hilary almost enjoyed a piano lesson.

At five o'clock the lesson was over. Waldo left the couch and approached the piano cautiously. "You know what?" he said, looking at his sister with awe. "It's just like Stevie's player-piano—only better." Stevie's parents had an old player-piano that played by itself when you pumped air into it, only instead of a person inside of it, the piano had paper rolls with holes punched in it for the notes.

The children were about to lift the lid of the piano and release Miss Orpheo, when they heard footsteps. Whirling around, they saw their mother standing in the doorway with a tray of dainty candy dishes, filled with nuts and pretty little thin mints. Although Mrs. Banister wore an apron over her dress, Hilary could tell from her mother's elaborate hair style that she had just returned from the beauty parlor.

"Why, Hilary, are you through with your lesson? I didn't realize Miss Orpheo had left already."

Hilary and Waldo glanced from their mother to the piano, and then looked down at the floor, trying to avoid her eyes. Hilary's cheeks were red. Waldo was the color of chalk. The piano, fortunately, was silent.

Mrs. Banister continued talking, all the while flitting about the room, straightening pictures, distributing the candy dishes, and turning lampshades so that the seams didn't show. "Children," she announced, "we are having dinner company tonight. Please keep your hands off the walls—they've just been cleaned. Waldo, throw your gum wrappers away and keep your sneakers in your room. Hilary, you left your hairbrush in the kitchen. Hang up your coats, put your books away, be polite, don't make noise, NO FIGHTING!" (she waved a finger at both of them), "do your homework, don't turn the TV too loud, take a bath, and," she paused to catch her breath, "oh yes, don't leave the bathroom looking like a swamp."

"Anything else," asked Waldo, his eyes twinkling.

"Yes, don't burn incense. It makes people sneeze." Waldo's hand reached toward the dish of nuts his mother had just set on the table. She snatched the dish away. "Waldo! There's a jar in the kitchen, if you want some." Mrs. Banister turned to the bookcase and began to rearrange the books, removing a few tattered paperback mysteries. As she turned to the piano, the children eyed their mother uneasily. Hilary sidled into the curve of the piano, draped her arms across the top, and stood there trying to look cool and casual.

"Who's coming tonight?" she asked, hoping to dis tract her mother.

Mrs. Banister set a dish of thin mints on the piano. "Oh, just a few friends. Madame Kunigunde will be here. Marylla Baynes . . ."

"You mean the one who wrote that dirty book?" Hilary interrupted. She was dying to meet the author of *Flesh*.

"It is not a dirty book," replied Mrs. Banister primly. "It is based on science: anthropology, to be precise." She examined a silver bowl to see if it needed polishing and flicked a dustcloth across the top of the piano. "Please, dear—move." Hilary didn't budge. For a moment Mrs. Banister hesitated. Then she looked at her watch and said, "Oh dear, I meant to vacuum the inside of the piano, but I guess there isn't enough time now. I'll have to do it some other time."

Hilary breathed a sigh of relief and moved away from the piano. Waldo gulped and looked across the room at Hilary. "Who else is coming?" he asked his mother.

"Well . . ." Mrs. Banister snipped a dead leaf from a plant and stared unhappily at the drapes. "I don't know when your father will get around to doing something about this house," she said half to herself. And then in answer to Waldo's question, she said brightly, "Well, Aunt Ottilie and Uncle Archer will be here."

"Yuch!" said Hilary.

"Double yuch!" said Waldo.

"Children—that's not nice," said Mrs. Banister. "Aunt Ottilie and Uncle Archer are very devoted to both of you."

"They're devoted to their precious Sally Anne," said Hilary. "Are they bringing her?"

"Of course not," said Mrs. Banister. "This is an adult party."

"I can't stand Sally Anne," said Hilary. "She thinks she's so great."

"Nonsense. Sally Anne's a sweet child. And very talented," said Mrs. Banister. "Now, I want both of you to be very good tonight." Mrs. Banister turned to her daughter. "And Hilary, you know what, dear . . ."

Here it comes, thought Hilary. Her mother did this every time they had company.

". . . it would be so nice, dear, if you would play something for us tonight. Just a little music before dinner. Besides, Aunt Ottilie and Uncle Archer haven't really heard you in so long."

"And they're not going to for even longer." Hilary made a face. "I don't have anything to play."

"Don't be silly, dear," laughed her mother. "I'm certain you will find something. Play one of your recital pieces. It will be good experience." And with a smile and a flick of her dustcloth, Mrs. Banister whisked off into the kitchen where Mrs. Caraway was putting the finishing touches on the *Filet de Boeuf*—a French version of roast beef. Ruining it, in Waldo's opinion.

The children waited until their mother was safely out of the room. They dashed to the piano, removed the candy dish, and together, lifted the top slightly. Hilary leaned over and whispered into it.

"Miss Orpheo, did you hear that?"

"I'm not deaf."

"Would you mind staying? I mean, we were going to let you out . . ."

"Really? How considerate of you."

"What I mean is . . ." Hilary hesitated and then continued, ". . . well, we don't expect you to stay in the piano forever, but, Oh God! you don't know what it's like having to play for all of them. Take my Aunt Ottilie . . ."

"*You* may take her," said Miss Orpheo.

"You don't know what she's like." Hilary groaned and mimicked her aunt: "'Hilary, dear, how nice your hair looks; so much better than usual.'"

"I have no intention of going," said Miss Orpheo. "I have not yet completed my investigation. Hmm. The felts seem to be in good condition. Undoubtedly, the piano has not been played that much." Miss Orpheo's voice sounded distant. It seemed to have dropped still farther down into the piano.

"Oh dear!" she murmured.

"Oh dear, what?" said Hilary.

"What's the matter?" asked Waldo.

The children stuck their noses into the piano, but it was dark and they couldn't see anything.

"Hapchoo! Haaapchoooooooo!" went Miss Orpheo.

"God bless you," said Hilary and Waldo.

"I'm certain He will," replied Miss Orpheo. "Gracious me, it *is* dusty in here."

Suddenly a little scale rippled up the piano—DO RE MI FA SOL—and abruptly stopped. Hilary dropped the lid of the piano with a thud, dashed around to the keyboard, and quickly covered the keys with her hands.

"Miss Orpheo, *please*, I mean, what would people think?"

Twank! Went the inside of the piano. *Hapchoo!* went Miss Orpheo.

Hilary and Waldo risked saying nothing.

"What's she doing?" asked Waldo, hopping up and down.

"Shh," said Hilary. She pointed toward the kitchen.

"Ask her what she wants to eat," suggested Waldo. "If she's going to stay in there, she might be getting hungry."

Leave it to Waldo, thought Hilary. His mind was in his stomach. Still, it was a good idea. She spoke into the opening behind the music rack. "Miss Orpheo, we thought you might be hungry. We'll be right back with a sandwich for you. The kitchen's sort of busy," she apologized. "Would tuna fish be O.K.?"

"I detest tuna fish."

"Peanut butter and jelly?" suggested Waldo hopefully.

Hilary poked him in the ribs. "Dope, she won't eat that."

"She certainly won't," came Miss Orpheo's faraway voice. "A carrot-and-cucumber sandwich would do very nicely," she said, "and if possible, a glass of lemonade."

"If we start making lemonade now, Mrs. Caraway will kill us," Hilary said hesitantly.

"That's not likely," said Miss Orpheo. "A cup of tea will do. With lemon—two slices, please. *Lemon aids in time of trial!* Mark what I say, Hilary."

"One tea with lemon, one carrot-and-cucumber sandwich coming up," piped Waldo, pouring a handful of nuts down his throat.

"Excellent," said Miss Orpheo. "And please bring a napkin. We don't want crumbs in our piano, do we? Crumbs bring moths. And moths . . ." The piano gave an alarmed rumble. ". . . moths wreak havoc with the felts."

"What's 'wreak havoc'?" asked Waldo as they chased into the kitchen to get Miss Orpheo's sandwich.

"A word you don't understand," Hilary answered.

Uh-oh! The ascending scale began playing again, continuing from where it had broken off before: LA TI DO, went the piano; then back down the scale, DO TI LA SOL FA MI . . .

Horrified, Hilary raced back to the living room and flung her arms over the piano. "Miss Orpheo, please! You mustn't do that."

No answer. Hilary eyed the piano suspiciously. She waited. The next note sounded: RE . . .

"PLEASE!" Hilary gave a muffled shriek. "They'll hear you, Miss Orpheo. You must promise to be good."

"Oh dear," said Miss Orpheo faintly. "I promise."

Cautiously, Hilary stepped away from the piano and turned toward the kitchen. She looked back at the piano nervously. It remained silent. Waldo put his hands in his pockets. He stuck his nose in the air and chuckled. Hilary hated Waldo when he went into his Smarty-pants act. "What's so funny?" she asked.

"Nothing. I was just thinking of something."

"Obviously," said Hilary annoyed. "C'mon, it's get-

ting late and we have work to do." Just as they got to
the kitchen, the piano sounded a single loud, firm note:
DO—the missing note in the interrupted scale. Hilary
sighed. "I guess she just *had* to finish it."

"Let's hope she doesn't start another," said Waldo.
"She really likes to play. You still didn't tell me what
'wreak havoc' means," he complained.

"Messed up, Waldo, messed up"—which is what the
kitchen was when they finally got there: pots, pans, plat-
ters, glasses, bowls, groceries, carrot tops, cucumber par-
ings, apple peels; meat roasting in the oven, things
steaming on top of the stove, other things being washed
in the sink; the mixer whirring and the exhaust fan
moaning—and in the midst of it all, Mrs. Caraway singing one of her cooking songs. Mrs. Caraway said singing
was good for the food. Hilary couldn't argue with that.
The kitchen smelled marvelous: warm and roasty, juicy
and sweet. Warily, she looked around for something to
taste.

"Young man, get your hand outa that," scolded Mrs.
Caraway, as Waldo dragged his finger through a bowl of
chocolate icing. "And don't you be picking them
grapes." She pulled Waldo's other hand out of the fruit
bowl.

"Why don't *we* get any?" he grumbled.

"Here." She handed them each a cookie. The doorbell
rang and Mrs. Caraway hurried to answer it. It was
Phoebe, the extra waitress engaged for the evening.
While Mrs. Caraway was outside talking to Phoebe,
Hilary grabbed a carrot and a cucumber, and then

headed for the bread box. Waldo got a plate and a knife.

"Quick, napkins!" said Hilary. Waldo ripped a flock of napkins out of the box just as Mrs. Caraway returned to the kitchen.

"What are you doing in them napkins?" she bellowed, pointing to the floor. Waldo made a face and scooted around the floor picking up the napkins. "Now you children get out from under my feet. I'll call you when supper's ready. Your mother said for me to fix you some hamburgers." With that, Mrs. Caraway slapped her dishtowel at them and shooed them past the oven where little pigs-in-blankets and crusty cheese wafers waited; past the tray of tiny, iced cakes, past the bowl of luscious fruit. Waldo reached for a grape. "Waldo!" Mrs. Caraway screamed at him. "Out! Out! Do you hear me? OUT!"

"O.K. O.K." they both yelled, laughing as Mrs. Caraway drove them out of her kitchen and closed the door behind them.

They stood clutching the ingredients of Miss Orpheo's supper.

"Where'll we go?" asked Waldo.

"Quick, follow me." Hilary had an idea. She led the way to the bathroom. It was a little cramped, but no worse than Mrs. Caraway's kitchen. And it had a lock. Safely inside, they locked the door and sat down on the floor to slice the carrot and cucumber for Miss Orpheo's sandwich.

"What about the tea?" asked Waldo, nibbling a piece of cucumber.

"We'll get it later," said Hilary. She looked up at Waldo and screamed, "You dope, you've eaten all the cucumber!"

"Make a plain carrot sandwich." Then he volunteered, "I could give her a piece of my bubble gum instead."

Hilary brandished the knife at him in disgust.

They put the sliced carrot on the bread. They cut the sandwich in half and put it on the plate. Then they tip-toed back to the kitchen. Fortunately, Mrs. Caraway was in the dining room arranging the wine glasses on the buffet table. Phoebe was busy in the pantry. Hilary filled a cup with hot water from the teakettle and added two slices of lemon she found already sliced in a bowl of shrimp. Waldo plopped a tea bag into the hot water. On the way out of the kitchen, Hilary helped herself to two fancy cookies. She put one in her mouth and one on the sandwich plate. Miss Orpheo's supper was now complete.

In the living room the piano remained silent.

11

THE PARTY

At five minutes to seven the doorbell rang. "Drat!" said Mr. Banister, who was shaving. "I told you someone would come early."

"Oh dear," said Mrs. Banister, "I haven't even got my face on." Hilary was perched on the edge of the bathtub, watching her mother apply her eye make-up. "Hilary dear," said Mrs. Banister, inspecting the eye she had just finished, "run and tell Mrs. Caraway to make whoever-it-is comfortable. Tell them I'll be right there." Hilary trudged inside to deliver her mother's message.

"I'm sorry I'm early," she heard the embarrassed guest apologize. Mrs. Caraway led the man into the living room, where he busied himself nibbling peanuts and leafing through the unabridged dictionary.

"It's Loris Adams," Hilary told her mother when she

returned. Loris Adams was a millionaire paper cup man-
ufacturer who liked to think of himself as an artist.

Mrs. Banister glanced nervously at herself in the mirror. "I guess I'm ready. I hate people who come early,"
she said to her husband. And then, turning to Hilary,
she explained, "You may come to a party a trifle late,
dear, but to arrive early is unforgivable. Remember
that."

Hilary looked at her mother with admiration. It took
Mrs. Banister forever "to put on her face," but the final
effect was a dramatic work of art. It was as if her
mother had finished painting in a face whose potential
charm she'd known about all the time. Mrs. Banister
was wearing the emerald earrings Hilary's father had
given her for their anniversary, and a long, shimmery
green gown. Her hair, piled in splendid curls on top of
her head, added an illusion of height. She looked beautiful, Hilary thought.

"Did you see my other shoe?" yelled Mr. Banister,
who was crawling around on his knees, one hand groping blindly under the bed. "Well, dammit!" he fumed,
"I'll just have to manage with one shoe." But nobody
heard his remark. Hilary had gone hunting for Waldo,
and Mrs. Banister had hurried inside to greet the single
guest, who was drifting uncomfortably around the
brightly lighted, too silent, too tidy living room.

A few minutes later the doorbell rang again: two
sharp, insistent staccatos. Mrs. Caraway opened the door
and in floated Aunt Ottilie, followed by Uncle Archer.
Aunt Ottilie greeted Mrs. Caraway without looking at

her and allowed her to take her coat. It sounded like at least five people.

Hilary and Waldo were watching from the kitchen pantry. "I wonder if they brought us anything?" said Waldo.

"Waldo!" Hilary pretended to sound shocked. "You are the most materialistic little kid I've ever met."

"I am NOT a little kid," Waldo protested, karate-chopping his sister's shoulder.

Hilary was about to bop him on the head when she heard her aunt's shrill voice: "Don't tell me the children are in bed already?"

"Of course not," replied Mrs. Banister. "Waldo! Hilary!" she called, hurrying toward the pantry. "Aunt Ottilie and Uncle Archer are here. Please come inside and say hello to them."

Reluctantly, they came forward to be looked over and evaluated. Like animals in a zoo, Hilary thought. She stared at her aunt and uncle and did a little evaluating of her own. Uncle Archer looked like a washed-out version of Hilary's father, who was his brother. To Hilary, it seemed as if someone had started out to make her father, had gotten a little vague and forgetful, and had instead produced Uncle Archer. Aunt Ottilie looked carved and painted. She was wearing her new diamond necklace. It looked like it was strangling her. Aunt Ottilie didn't look like an aunt—at least not the way aunts were supposed to look. She looked like somebody's worst friend.

"My, Hilary, you look very pretty," said Aunt Ottilie.

131

"You've gained a little weight, haven't you? I must say, it's becoming."

Hilary wanted to kill her.

"Where's Waldo?" she asked, spinning away from Hilary. "Ah . . . here's our little man."

Waldo winced and held his breath while Aunt Ottilie chucked him under the chin and ran her hand through his soft brown hair. Hilary and Waldo glanced at each other, disgusted. What did they think Waldo was? A cocker spaniel?

"Here's a little box of candy for you," said Aunt Ottilie, thrusting an enormous box of plump chocolates into Waldo's hands. "Now, don't eat it all at once," she said, laughing.

"That's right," chuckled Uncle Archer, "don't eat it all at once."

Aunt Ottilie was talking to Hilary's mother. "Lydia dear, everything looks simply glorious. Come, I want to see the couch you had redone." And with that, they all moved into the living room to join poor Mr. Adams, who was eating his way through the peanuts.

Quickly, Hilary and Waldo tore open the gorgeous box of chocolates.

"Eeeech! They're filled with rum," Hilary screamed as she ran to spit hers out. "I hate that kind."

"Me too," said Waldo, dropping his sticky half-eaten chocolate into a convenient candy dish.

"It's just what you'd expect from them," said Hilary. Together, the children went back to their nook in the pantry to watch the rest of the guests arrive.

The doorbell rang again. Madame Kunigunde entered

in a huge fur coat that reached almost to her ankles. In one hand she carried a silly little beaded handbag; in the other, a battered paper shopping bag. "It *is* tonight . . . the party? I am expected?" She entered the apartment and began to extract herself from the tremendous coat. "The mink you may haff," she said rolling out of it and handing it to Mrs. Caraway. "Poor dear, he is not much mink left," she laughed, patting the coat affectionately. "But this I keep," and reaching deep into the shopping bag, she brought forth a thin folder. "I haff brought with me zome little zongs. Maybe later I will zing," she clucked.

"Why, that would be simply lovely!" exclaimed Mrs. Banister.

Madame Kunigunde rummaged around in the shopping bag and pulled out three bags of candy: chocolate kisses, miniature chocolate bars, and little Tootsie Rolls. "I haff not the time to wrap it," she apologized to a grateful Waldo, who had popped into the room just in time to accept the wonderful Woolworth candy. Waldo thanked Madame Kunigunde and scurried back to his lair in the pantry to show Hilary their good fortune.

Ring! went the doorbell. Mr. and Mrs. Claxton. Mrs. Claxton was wearing something that looked like a long see-through nightgown.

Ring! The Amongettis. Hilary's father had done a house for them. Mr. Amongetti was a lawyer; his wife was, well, his wife. She seemed very timid and hung on her husband's arm like an umbrella.

Next a whole bunch of people Hilary had never seen

before arrived, followed by the Quinns. Mrs. Quinn worked with Hilary's mother on a committee to keep people from making wild animals into fur coats and pocketbooks.

Ring! Again, ring! And then, Ring! Ring! Ring!

"Wow!" said Waldo. "There's lots of them."

"Yeah," said Hilary. "I don't see how they know so many people."

The party guests arrived in clusters. Hilary noticed a woman in shoes that looked like high-heeled sneakers. As the conversation gained momentum, the living room grew crowded and noisy. Mr. Banister, smiling and handsome, fixed drinks for his friends, while Mrs. Banister, looking radiant, floated about introducing people to one another. Hilary found it hard to believe that this beautiful, flirtatious woman in the long, green gown was the same woman—her mother—who washed dishes, worked at the hospital, marketed, put them to bed at night, and did all the drab, household things mothers had to do. She noticed the admiring glance her father gave her mother.

It's funny, Hilary thought, how different one's parents acted at a party. They weren't parents; they were strangers. And why, Hilary wondered, is that man with the mustache kissing my mother? Where was her father? There he was. Oh, wow! Hilary's eyes popped. Her father was kissing an absolutely gorgeous-looking blonde in a stunning silver jumpsuit made of . . . ?

"Did you see THAT?" Hilary gasped at Waldo. "She has nothing on underneath!"

"How do you know?"

"I'm not blind."

"Hilary! Hilareee!" Over the din, Hilary heard her mother's voice calling. A man had just walked in, balancing a huge bundle of flowers over his shoulder. "Oh, there you are, Hilary," said Mrs. Banister, handing Hilary the flowers. "Be a dear," she said prettily in her special company voice, "and take these beautiful flowers inside to Mrs. Caraway. She'll find a vase for you."

Her mother was a good actress. In addition to people who arrived early at dinner parties, Mrs. Banister hated people who brought flowers at the last moment, especially enormous, long-stemmed flowers for which you might not have a vase.

"Lord, love us! What now?" bawled Mrs. Caraway when she saw Hilary. She found a heavy vase for the tall red gladiolas, and Hilary returned with them to her mother.

"Where shall I put them?"

Mrs. Banister looked around. The room was already filled with the charming flower arrangements she had done for the party. "Right there—on the piano." Mrs. Banister took the heavy vase from Hilary and set it down on top of Miss Orpheo.

While everyone admired the flowers, Mrs. Quinn edged her way over to inspect Hilary. Hilary braced herself. "My, how she's grown! She's going to be tall, Lydia," said Mrs. Quinn, running her eyes up and down Hilary as if she were a piece of meat. What did they expect? Hilary wondered. Mrs. Quinn hadn't seen her in a year. She couldn't just stay *still*.

"She's going to have a good figure, too," the woman snickered.

Hilary fled. Why did certain people talk about you as if you weren't there?

She found Waldo in his room sitting on his bed in a storm of torn wrapping paper. "Mom said I could open them," he said, anticipating Hilary's question.

They examined the loot:

One box of horrible rum-filled chocolates from You-Know-Who. Three bags of candy from Madame Kunigunde (terrific!). Two bottles of wine (blech!). One box of cookies with pink centers. (Mmm. They sighed happily, sampling them.) *"Mother Goose?* They've got to be kidding!" exclaimed Hilary, unwrapping a book of nursery rhymes. "How old do they think we are?"

"Hey, look at this!" yelled Waldo. There were three beautifully wrapped packages, labeled *For Waldo, For Hilary, For Lydia and Simon*—"from their good friend, Marylla Baynes." The children tore open the paper.

"Wow! Oh wow!" shrieked Waldo. His package contained a heavy wooden slingshot. "Wait'll Stevie sees this!"

"Wait'll Mom sees it," muttered Hilary, ripping the paper from her own package. She held her breath and pulled out a fantastic leather belt. It was covered with tiny glass jewels and had a heavy buckle. "And we don't even know her." It was funny how some people knew just what you wanted, even if they had never met you.

Just then Mrs. Banister stuck her head into the room. "Children, I want you to come and meet Marylla Baynes. She's been asking for you."

Hilary was eager to meet Marylla Baynes. To have written a book like *Flesh*, a person must have really lived.

What a crushing blow. Marylla Baynes was a dumpy little woman, wearing a fussy blue dress that showed the flab on her arms. Her gray hair had been set in a stiff circle of frozen curls, by a hairdresser skilled at making his customers look awful. Although disappointing as a sex symbol, Marylla Baynes turned out to be just as nice as her gifts. She chatted pleasantly with Hilary about the problems of writing books, and made Hilary blush with pleasure by telling her that she had beautiful hair.

The pre-dinner rhythm of the party accelerated. People talked and nibbled delicious tidbits passed to them on a silver tray by Phoebe. Loris Adams, confident and at ease now, conversed earnestly with a tall woman who painted pictures you couldn't see.

Uncle Archer had wandered off to a corner where he sat staring morosely into his drink. Uncle Archer always got depressed at parties. Aunt Ottilie was flitting about the room, chatting, chirping, occasionally alighting on the arm of a chair. Hilary noticed that her aunt always looked past people when she talked to them.

Momentarily, the chatter died down. "Lydia, darling!" Aunt Ottilie's voice soared across the room, "I see you've finally re-covered that ghastly armchair. I hope you have better luck with that fabric than we did. I

used it in Sally Anne's room and it disintegrated—
completely. Just fell apart."

Waldo gave Hilary a shove. "That's cause Sally Anne
lives in the room," he snickered. Hilary giggled, too.

In the living room, someone dandled his fingers over
the piano keys. It sounded a few notes and for an instant the din in the room subsided.

"Oh Madame Kunigunde," warbled Mrs. Claxton, glid-
ing over to the piano, "*do* say you are going to treat us
to some music tonight?"

Madame Kunigunde gave forth a deep, throaty cluck.
"I should not zing—but you haff talked it into me. But
later, my children, after Lydia's mahvelous zupper."

Brrroooong! KRONK! An ear-splitting crunch of
chords sounded from the piano. Hilary spun around,
stunned, and then breathed a sigh of relief. It was only
Loris Adams who accidentally had sat down on the
piano keys. Poor Miss Orpheo. Hilary hoped she hadn't
been taken by surprise.

Mrs. Banister glanced around the room for an instant,
her eyes darting in and out, looking for something . . .

Hilary's stomach froze. "Here it comes," she said to
herself. In spite of everything, she began to shake.

"Hilary, dear," said Mrs. Banister, finding her mark at
last, "it would be so lovely if you would play a little
something for us." She laughed, sounding pleased. "A
little *prelude* to dinner, shall we call it?" Her mother
spoke as if the idea had just dropped into her head out
of the blue.

"Hilary studies at the Henrietta St. George Music

School," Mrs. Banister explained, as if that were a guarantee of a rare musical treat. Hilary turned crimson. Whenever her mother wanted to impress people, she would say, "Hilary studies." The rest of the time, Hilary just "took piano lessons." Why did her mother have to use her to show off? Or at least, why didn't she pick something Hilary was good at—like tennis? You couldn't play tennis at a dinner party, of course, but . . .

"Hilary?" Her mother stood smiling at her.

Hilary looked at the piano. Miss Orpheo was inside, waiting patiently. "I don't know anything," she mumbled, automatically falling into her usual routine for this scene.

"Oh, play anything," suggested Mrs. Banister brightly. "How about that little Mozart thing—you know, the one that goes . . ." She hummed a few notes.

"I don't have that any more," said Hilary sullenly. "Besides, it isn't Mozart. It's Haydn."

"Then play the Bach, dear," said her mother. "It's pretty, and not too long. It *is* Bach, isn't it?" she inquired.

Hilary nodded miserably. She took her seat at the piano. People went right on talking, drinking, and oh-my-dearing. Suddenly, without warning, the piano struck two angry chords.

YIKES! Hilary jerked her hands across the keyboard, trying to approximate the chords. What was Miss Orpheo up to?

Trouble—that's what. The room grew quiet, and for an instant all eyes turned toward Hilary. Even her parents looked startled. Then, without waiting for Hilary,

Miss Orpheo swung into a spirited performance of the Bach Invention. Hilary followed at the keyboard, doing her best to keep up. Never mind if Hilary missed a note, Miss Orpheo was there. If Hilary forgot the F-sharp in line five, Miss Orpheo was there. If Hilary's fingers tangled, no matter—Miss Orpheo pressed on. La-di da-di-DA . . . Oh, how they played! Right past the Horrible Spot, and safely through the tricky closing passage where the two voices came together (and Hilary usually came apart). Her fingers rested. It was over. The astonished audience burst into enthusiastic applause.

"Bravo!" shouted Madame Kunigunde, her hands extended in front of her great bosom, clapping heartily. Waddling over to the piano, she embraced Hilary and pressed a squishy kiss on her head. "Lydia, you are very naughty," she scolded. "You haff never told me the child was so ta-LEN-ted. Play zumzing more," she commanded.

Hilary began to shake her head. Enough was enough. But inside the piano, down under the hammers and dampers, Miss Orpheo had other ideas. She began the Mazurka. There was nothing for Hilary to do but attend to her part at the keyboard and watch the pedal.

Hey, wait . . . HEY! Something was wrong. My God! thought Hilary, what's she playing? It sounded like a mazurka, but it wasn't Hilary's mazurka. Frantically, Hilary bent over her hands, nose down to the keys, pretending to be deeply involved in her playing. Using her body as a shield, she tried to keep people from seeing her hands, which had no idea what notes to play. The mazurka (or whatever it was) continued playing itself, becoming increasingly complicated. The whole thing was wild! This time Miss Orpheo had gone too far. What was the matter with the woman? Hoping that the huge flowers would hide her, Hilary lifted from her seat slightly and leaned into the piano behind the music rack.

"Where *are* you?" she whispered desperately.

"In the piano," came the faint, somewhat breathless answer.

Hilary almost strangled. "No . . . I mean . . . in the *music?*"

"Second repeat, third measure . . . ooops! fourth measure."

This was no time for jokes. Hilary was ready to scream, but she had to keep her hands busy, pretending to play. She leaned into the piano again.

"What *piece?*" she hissed at Miss Orpheo.

This time Miss Orpheo seemed to understand. The lilting melody dissolved, carried off in streaks of scale-work. The music thickened, becoming heavy with notes. Hilary hunched over the keyboard, trying bravely to follow a curious series of chord progressions—the musical bridge by which Miss Orpheo intended to escape from the strange mazurka. And go? Hilary shuddered and held her breath. After all, Chopin wrote tons of mazurkas! Finally, Miss Orpheo emerged from the network of harmonies, and breaking into a long galloping trill, pivoted and landed gracefully in Hilary's mazurka.

Whew!

Hilary breathed a sigh of relief as the familiar notes began to rise and fall under her fingers. At last, it was safe to press the keys. She lifted her nose from the keyboard and sat erect. Then, relaxed and confident, she played on serenely to the end of the piece, thoroughly enjoying her triumph.

The room was silent for a moment, and then everybody began clapping wildly. Flushed with pleasure and embarrassment, Hilary looked over the guests' heads, scanning the room, searching for Waldo. She found him, just behind the living-room door. Catching his eye, she winked. Waldo winked back, and shook his clasped hands over his head in a sign of victory.

It was over, and now Hilary only wanted one thing: to escape. Carefully, she arose and moved away from the piano. Please, Miss Orpheo, she prayed inwardly, don't play any more. Miss Orpheo seemed to be enjoying herself a little too much for comfort. It occurred to Hilary that her teacher might decide to play Hilary's entire repertoire, not to mention compositions (like the strange mazurka) Hilary had never heard of. She glanced uneasily at the keys, but meek and obedient, the piano remained silent.

Aunt Ottilie, eyes gleaming, drink in hand, rushed up to Hilary. "Hilary, darling, you certainly *are* making progress!" she gushed. "I've always loved that perfectly beautiful nocturne. Sally Anne used to play it . . . when she was—oh so little."

"It's not a nocturne," said Hilary through clenched teeth. "It's a mazurka." Hilary thought she heard the piano rumble. It was probably only her imagination.

"Mazurka . . . nocturne . . . it's all the same to me," said Uncle Archer with his usual hearty laugh. He was about to say something else, when Mrs. Banister announced that dinner was ready, whereupon the guests, led by Uncle Archer who adored food, wound their way into the dining room.

"Hilary, dear," said Mrs. Banister, beaming at her daughter, "that was lovely—indeed, unexpectedly lovely. Go take your bath now—and, oh yes, tell Waldo to wear pajamas," she added.

Mr. Banister paused in front of Hilary and gave his daughter a hard, searching look. He didn't say anything. Then he patted her on the head and followed his guests into the dining room.

The minute the coast was clear, Waldo appeared from behind the living-room door. They dashed to the piano.

"We'd better let her out," said Waldo.

"She *is* out," said Hilary. "Look!"

The lid of the piano had been raised slightly and was left propped open by a book. Hilary looked startled. It was *Fossil in the Frigidaire*. Miss Orpheo's supper dishes were on the piano bench. The vase of red gladiolas stood on the floor. Cautiously, the children peeked into the piano.

"Look! There's a note," cried Hilary. On the strings spanning the soundboard lay a piece of paper covered with Miss Orpheo's handwriting. Hilary pulled the paper out and began to read:

Dear Hilary and Waldo:

I am sorry I could not wait, but I dislike traveling about the city after dark. (One can't be too careful these days!) It is very pleasant and uplifting inside your piano, and I daresay we shall at last master that wretched passage in the Bach so that you don't stumble over it.

In case you are wondering why I have chosen to co-operate

with your plans—that is for me to know, and you to wonder. Suffice it to say, I have not had a vacation in a long time. I loathe sandy, buggy places; I also detest the mountains. It is very restful and inspiring in here, and the atmosphere is conducive to peaceful contemplation and to steeping oneself in the spirit of music. At the same time, you too may profit.

Moreover, the piano was designed neither for the performance of "Chopsticks" nor to serve as a flower pedestal. The piano is the servant of music. But only music! It pleases me to enable this majestic instrument to serve the purpose for which it was intended. All of us come at last to our true vocation.

"What's she talking about?" sputtered Waldo.

"Be quiet. Listen to this." Hilary turned the paper to the other side:

I shall await you on Wednesday at the St. George School. Naturally, I shall have assumed my new station inside the piano. The instrument in room 310 does not compare with your excellent Steinway. Yet, I have no doubt, it will be grateful for my attention. Inasmuch as I expect to assist you at your recital . . .

Hilary and Waldo exchanged glances.

. . . you are to PRACTICE VERY CAREFULLY! Your fingerwork must be impeccable.

"What's that mean?" asked Waldo.

"Stop interrupting," said Hilary, and went on reading:

Remember, Madame St. George will be listening. She is nobody's fool. And she is not blind. You must be able to play the notes perfectly. Beyond that, if you COUNT, you may count on me. I regret my oversight in the mazurka. The Opus 30, B-minor Mazurka belongs to my next pupil. Yours, as you

know, is in C-minor. Both beautiful works, I might add. Nonetheless, people who play together must stay together.

Lest you forget, we have a recital two weeks from Saturday.
WORK!

Yours faithfully,
Priscilla Orpheo

Hilary and Waldo stood speechless, staring at each
other, letting Miss Orpheo's words sink in. Slowly, carefully, Hilary folded Miss Orpheo's note and tore it in
half. In half again. She stuffed the pieces in her pocket.
Waldo removed the book from the piano and closed the
lid. Hilary returned the vase of flowers to the top of the
piano—feeling a trifle guilty about the ring mark. Finally, Waldo found his voice.

"Wait'll I tell Stevie," he gasped. "I'm going to call
him right now."

"You'll do nothing of the sort, Waldo Banister,"
Hilary ordered. "If you breathe a word of this to anybody, I'll take back the comics I gave you."

"You already took them back," said Waldo. "Besides,
if I can't tell Stevie, then you can't tell Cookie. It's only
fair."

Hilary looked thoughtful. "Look, dumbhead, suppose
I call Cookie . . ."

"Yeah?"

"May I ask precisely *what* you think I'm going to tell
her?"

An hour later Hilary lay in her bed, thinking about
everything that had happened. Through the closed door

she could hear the muted sounds of the party. Great male *ho-ho-ho's!* boomed out; shrill female voices piped above the drone of conversation. At one point the room grew quiet. The piano sounded and Madame Kunigunde began to sing. It sounded like somebody being scalped, Hilary thought. Imagine *wanting* to perform for people! Hilary pulled the quilt up over her shoulders and snuggled down beneath it. She closed her eyes and drifted toward sleep.

Out of the swirl of silent forms, slowed-up thoughts, and detached words, there took shape a vast stage. In the center stood a gleaming concert grand piano, its great wing top raised, poised for flight. Hilary saw herself glide across the stage in a long, emerald-green gown. She bowed to the audience and took her seat at the piano. No one breathed. She began to play the Bach Invention, her fingers dancing light as the wind over the keys. As she played, an orchestra appeared at the foot of the stage and gradually the modest little Invention became a noble piano concerto. Whirlwind runs, thundering octaves, and crystalline trills poured from her fingers. Her extended arms seemed to grow longer and longer, embracing the entire piano, making it part of her. An exquisite melody, embroidered in the sumptuous texture of the music, wove its way, soaring and singing. The audience listened in wonder, deeply moved by the luminous beauty of Hilary's playing.

Then, while the concerto continued, Hilary watched herself rise and bow. Looking across the footlights, she saw Madame St. George wiping tears from her eyes, gazing up at her with awe. She saw Lyra Lyons and Miss

Edgeworth and a whole group of pupils and parents from the school. Aunt Ottilie was there, sitting in the audience with Uncle Archer and precious Sally Anne. She saw Madame Kunigunde and someone who was Marylla Baynes, but didn't look like her. The Claxtons were there, applauding like mad, and her parents . . . Madame St. George came forward, floating down the aisle toward Hilary, her arms outstretched. But it wasn't the audience; it wasn't the applause, or even the look on Aunt Ottilie's face that mattered. To her surprise, these things no longer seemed important.

The orchestra began to fade, and the simpler notes of the Bach Invention returned. As these too dissolved into silence, Hilary finally understood what it was she yearned for: to be BEST—best at something; to know the joy and power of doing something better than anyone else. If you could do that, then you could really see and feel yourself. You could be certain that you were somebody—that you existed. There was something else, too, but the dream shifted out of focus. Hilary rolled over on her pillow and gave a little shiver as a sigh escaped from her.

When Mrs. Banister tiptoed into the room a little later, the concert stage was gone, the audience had departed, and Hilary was sound asleep.

12

THE MORNING OF
THE DAY

On the morning of the piano recital, Hilary awoke at six o'clock and sat bolt upright in bed. It was dark. A strange hush hung in the air, a silence so insistent it demanded attention. Shivering in the chilly room, Hilary hopped out of bed and went to the window. The first snow of winter had fallen, erasing the dirty, gray city. It covered the street, window ledges, rooftops, lampposts, trash pails, and cars; it covered everything in a clean, silent blanket of white. The night before, the city on the edge of winter had looked drab and old. Now it looked like fairyland.

Hilary smiled with delight as she gazed up the street at the beautiful snow, unbroken except for a few tire marks. The lumbering buses, groaning and screeching at each start and stop, sounded muffled and far away. In the distance, Hilary could hear the anguished whine of an automobile wheel spinning on the slippery ground. A man walked down the middle of the deserted street.

Hilary jumped back into bed and snuggled deep down under the warm covers. The room was getting light. Soon the city, its life suspended during the snowy night, would revive and the white snow would turn to dirty slush. But for a little longer, the snow and the sleepy dark would last. Hilary hugged herself under the warm quilt and closed her eyes. Then, abruptly, she woke up all over again and realized what day it was.

"Eat your breakfast, dear," said Mrs. Banister. "*Especially* today."

"I'm not hungry." Hilary's stomach had drawn itself into a tight, hard knot and was bouncing all over her insides.

"Hilary!" cried Mrs. Banister. "Look what you're doing!"

Hilary looked. She was tearing her toast into little shreds and depositing the pieces all over the table.

"Hilary's nervous," announced Waldo, biting a hole out of the center of his toast. He began to twirl the toast on the end of his finger.

"Waldo! Stop playing with your food." Mrs. Banister took the toast away from him. "Cut it with a knife, Waldo, and please chew!"

"I am," Waldo pouted. He took a sip of milk, leaned his head back, and began to gargle.

Hilary jumped up from the table and screamed, "MOTHHHER! Make him stop that. It's revolting!"

This made Waldo laugh, and the milk came spraying out of his mouth all over everything.

"WAAALLLDO!" moaned Mrs. Banister. "Now see what you've done!"

"PIG!" screamed Hilary and ran off to her room.

Waldo was pleading that he hadn't meant to do it—somehow the milk just got away from him. Mrs. Banister was trying to mop up the milk from the table, and the floor, and the walls, and the ceiling, when Mr. Banister came into the room and said, "Snow. Damn! I'll have to dig the car out."

"Well, today's the day," said Mrs. Banister brightly, setting her husband's juice and coffee in front of him.

"Sure is," said Waldo, slicing his throat with his finger. "What time is the concert?"

"What concert?" asked Mr. Banister.

"Hilary's recital . . . at the St. George School," said Mrs. Banister. "Why, Simon dear, you haven't forgotten? We're all going—at three o'clock. The Claxtons will be there, too. They're on the Board of Trustees."

Waldo made a face and stuck his finger into the toaster.

"Waldo!" cried Mrs. Banister, yanking his hand out of the toaster. "Do you want to get electrocuted?"

"Uh-huh," said Waldo cheerfully.

"Actually," continued Mrs. Banister to her husband, "Hilary's worked very hard the past two weeks. As a matter of fact, I've never seen her practice so much."

"Mmm," said Mr. Banister. "Is there more coffee?"

The children taking part in the recital were expected at the music school an hour earlier, so they could draw lots to determine when they would play and listen to Madame St. George's "Don't Hurry—Don't Worry" pep talk. In the awful hours between the breakfast Hilary didn't eat and the lunch she didn't eat, Hilary decided to:

run away

have a nervous breakdown

take poison

break the sad news to her parents that she was completly paralyzed and could never again play the piano. (Really, her fingers *were* paralyzed. She tried to wiggle them. See . . . SEE . . . they didn't work!)

Then she rememberd Miss Orpheo. It wasn't last year; it was this year, she told herself. Things would be different. She had even practiced an hour and a half a day! Her fingers began to move and she felt better.

She telephoned Cookie.

"How *are* you?" Cookie asked.

"Horrible. I'll never live through it." Cookie was lucky. Her recital wasn't until next month. She was playing a violin and piano sonata with her teacher. If Cookie developed amnesia, or dropped the violin, at least Mr. Raelli would be there to carry on.

"What are you wearing to yours?" Hilary asked.

"My new dress . . . the one I got for Lisa's party."

"I've got to wear that sick green thing," Hilary groaned. "You know, the one with the pleats. My mother's making me. She says I picked it, so now I have to wear it."

"*You* picked that?" Cookie sounded shocked.

"Yeah, that was *then*. How could I tell my taste would change?"

"Stick a belt on it," Cookie suggested. "It won't look so stupid."

"You hope," muttered Hilary.

"Cheer up," said Cookie sympathetically. "You only die once."

It was almost two o'clock. Hilary was brushing her hair.

"Why, that dress looks nice with a belt," said Mrs. Banister. "Rather grown-up, I'd say."

Hilary nodded. The inside of her mouth was coated with paste. She felt lightheaded and wispy, as if all the solid substance had blown out of her. She didn't feel like Hilary.

"Here, dear, let me brush the back of your hair—you missed a spot," said Mrs. Banister, taking the brush. When she finished brushing, she stood back and inspected her daughter critically. She frowned.

"Hilary! Those shoes! They look terrible. Where are your good shoes?"

"Oh, Mom, these are good enough."

Mrs. Banister hesitated and then let it pass. "Did you cut your fingernails?"

Hilary nodded.

"Are they clean?"

"Yes."

"Oh yes, Hilary, put a clip in your hair so it won't fall in your eyes."

"I like it in my eyes."

"Not while playing, I'm sure," said Mrs. Banister.

Hilary made a face. She rummaged in her dresser drawer, found a gold clip and stabbed it into her hair.

"That's so much better," said Mrs. Banister. "Now we can see your face."

"Who wants to!" said Hilary irritably. Why didn't her mother leave her alone.

"What time shall we be there?" Mrs. Banister asked.

"Never," said Hilary unhappily. "Do you have to come?" Even with Miss Orpheo in the piano to help her, Hilary didn't think she could make it. She remembered last year and shuddered.

"Don't be silly," said her mother. "Of course we do. We're looking forward to it."

Why did they have to lie, Hilary wondered. Her father, she knew, was definitely not looking forward to it.

"In fact," continued Mrs. Banister, "this time we're *really* looking forward to it. Especially after the way you played at our party two weeks ago. Why, Hilary, it didn't even sound like *you*."

Hilary flinched. Her mother meant it as a compliment, of course. But it hurt. She couldn't blame her mother. How could she know about Miss Orpheo in the piano. Hilary Banister without Miss Orpheo was a musical moron; *with* Miss Orpheo . . . well . . .

"Even Waldo's coming," said Mrs. Banister, eyeing her daughter's dress. "He surprised me by asking to come—after all that talk about never going to another recital again."

"Yeah, I know."

"Hilary," said Mrs. Banister, still staring at Hilary's dress, "that dress . . . it's awfully short with the belt."

"MOOOTHER!" screamed Hilary. "Leave me alone."

Mrs. Banister took a step back. She looked hurt. When Hilary finally was ready to leave, she went to the door with her.

"'Bye Mom," said Hilary buttoning her coat.

"Have you got your gloves?"

"Yes."

"And a hat?"

"Nope."

"Wear your boots, Hilary. It's slushy outside."

"I don't need boots."

"Then at least wear a sweater."

"No!" Hilary rang for the elevator. What did a sweater have to do with her feet?

Mrs. Banister had nothing left to say, so she kissed her daughter and said, "Hurry, dear, you'll be late."

"'Bye, Mom," said Hilary. "Wish me luck." She looked around at her home for one last time, like someone going off never to return.

"Good luck, dear—and don't worry," said Mrs. Banister, sounding worried. "Be careful going over there, Hilary. Don't hurry. You have plenty of time."

Hilary stepped into the elevator and pressed the button. With a thud, the elevator settled at the ground floor. Hilary gave a start and suddenly remembered what she had forgotten.

Plip, plip, plip! She stabbed the number 15 button. The automatic elevator wasn't interested in Hilary's problems. It took its time. It knew its orders. The door

opened slowly and waited eight seconds before responding to the next request. Hilary banged on the "Close"
button and on number 15 at the same time. Eventually,
the elevator closed itself and began the ascent. It
stopped on the seventh floor. A man got on who wanted
to go *down*. The elevator carried him *up*. Hilary was furious at the man, at the idiotic elevator. . . . Annoyed,
the man stared into space over Hilary's head, as if he really didn't care where the elevator took him. Hilary
fumed, and fumbled in her pocket for her house key. Finally, they reached the fifteenth floor. She rammed the
key into the front door, opened it, and dashed inside.

"Is that you, Hilary?" Mrs. Banister called from her
room, where she was getting dressed.

"Yeah, I forgot something." She burst into Waldo's
room. "Waldo, the magic spell! I almost forgot. I know
it's dumb, but I can't go without it—especially today."

Waldo was watching television. "When my program's
over."

"Are you kidding?" screamed Hilary. "Waldo! Now!
C'mon," and grabbing her brother's arm she pulled him
into the living room.

"But you've got *her!*" said Waldo. "She'll be there,
won't she? In the piano?"

"I know, I know," Hilary said, "but say the spell, anyway." She collapsed in the Prayer Position in front of
the piano. Her bulky coat squashed itself up under her
chin, smothering her. "Quick, Waldo, I haven't got all
night. And please make it good," she pleaded. "I'll need
it."

Waldo nodded and began the ritual:

"Brahms, Beethoven, Mozart, Gluck," he intoned. *"God bless Hilary and bring her LUCK!"* He gave the air an extra swoosh with his arms.

Hilary looked up, surprised. So Waldo had been thinking about it, after all. He'd changed the words. She rather liked this version. She started to thank him.

"Hilll-aaa-reee!" called her mother, hurrying toward the living room.

Hilary bounced to her feet, straightened her coat, and gave her hair a shake.

"Is that you? Are you still here?" her mother called.

"No," shouted Hilary and ran out the door.

13

Time of Trial

Brrr. By the time Hilary got to the music school, she was almost frozen. The temperature was dropping rapidly in the waning daylight hours of the short winter afternoon. The morning snow and slush had begun to freeze into hard rivulets of ice. For a moment before going in, Hilary hesitated and took a last envious look up the street at the Outside World.

Elegantly dressed women in boots and fur hats darted in and out of the attractive shops lining the avenue. Little old ladies carrying heavy packages moved along carefully, muttering darkly at two boys hurling ice-snowballs across the street at each other. People hurrying north, people hurrying south; dogs pulling people, people pulling dogs. Shovels scraped, trucks rumbled and clattered, and cars crunched through the slippery streets, honking impatiently. Hilary felt a great wave of affection for these busy Saturday people—even the little old ladies.

The next time I stand here, she told herself, it will all be over. I'll be FREE. She gave herself a little shake. When you thought about Time, it was really weird. Eventually everything came; eventually everything went. It was comforting to know that nothing could last forever—even piano recitals. A group of laughing, joking boys and girls, ice skates strung about their necks, came swinging down the street, headed for the park. What a waste of an afternoon, Hilary thought sadly, and went inside.

If it was cold outside the music school, it was—in a different way—even colder inside. It gave Hilary the shivers. The gloomy, dark reception hall was already choked with people who had arrived early because of the snow. Vases of droopy bargain flowers had been set about the cavernous hall in an attempt to make the school look festive. Instead, the place looked like a funeral parlor—a noisy one. Hilary fixed her thoughts on Miss Orpheo and tried to keep this year's recital from sliding into last year's disaster. It was difficult. So much was the same: the school, the teachers, the stupid, stuck-up people.

Pressing through the crowd, she headed for the coat-room. The building resounded with the clamor of children's high-pitched voices, of nervous teachers patting their entries on the back, and of parents, guests, and friends milling about the reception hall. Skittish pupils in little clusters were asking where they should go and what they should do. Parents (mothers, actually) clutching programs greeted each other, twittering nervously. "How nice to see you!" "How marvelous!" "Is he, really? How perfectly awful!"

"How sickening!" muttered Hilary as she shoved her way into the coatroom, where it was even worse. The place was jammed with coats and people—happy, yappy music students who all knew and adored one another. It wasn't that Hilary was unfriendly or hadn't tried making friends. But people either hurried off, ignoring her timid "Hi!" or they nodded politely and went on talking to one another. Hilary stuck her coat on a hook over somebody else's coat, ran a comb nervously through her hair, and rubbed her frozen fingers. "Wear gloves," her mother's voice came back to her. As usual, her mother was right.

Since there was nothing else for Hilary to do in the stifling coatroom, she made her way back to the front hall and stood for a moment in the midst of the festive throng, awkward and alone, a stranger in her own music school. A woman, waving a program and screaming, "Geraldeeen, darling!" marched over Hilary's foot, bumping her with the sharp metal corner of her pocketbook. It hurt. A lump rose in Hilary's throat. She felt like crying. She thought of Miss Orpheo waiting for her in the piano. She wished she could hide in the piano, too.

It was all so stupid. In this room-size world of music lovers, doting parents, and musical geniuses, there was no place for Hilary. The only advantage of the crowd,

Hilary realized, was that people couldn't see how alone she was. She also hoped that nobody would recognize her and remember what had happened last year. Fortunately, she had grown taller and looked older now. If only Cookie were here, she thought, and glanced at her watch. Cookie had a dentist appointment and wouldn't make it until just before the recital. Her parents, of course, would be late—they always were.

Looking around, she noticed Lyra Lyons, smug and confident, in a corroded orange dress that showed her bulges. Hilary made her way through the crowd and said a shy hello to the fat girl. After all, she did know her from school. But Lyra Lyons didn't hear. Standing in the center of an admiring crowd, she was being worked over by her trainers. Her piano teacher was busy giving her last-minute instructions. Lyra's mother kept plumping out the awful orange velvet dress and tugging at Lyra's wiry hair, while Lyra's father, a little round man, went around patting Lyra on the back and on the head, and talking to all the people who pressed around squealing how wonderful Lyra looked. Lyra Lyons was a fat dope in school, but at a music recital she was a princess.

Hilary fidgeted with the belt of her dress. It was hard to believe that she actually envied Lyra Lyons. "Idiots! Snobs!" she sneered—because she was frightened and lonely and had no one to talk to. In school, and everywhere else, she was a normal member of the human race. She was good at schoolwork, tennis, and drawing. She was vice-president of the student council. But here, in this miserable, rotten music school, Hilary felt like a deformed, creepy monster: unfit, unwelcome, and at times invisible. The only reason the school kept her, she'd decided long ago, was because her parents paid the tuition and Madame St. George wasn't one to turn down money.

Well, they might just be surprised today—if she lived through it. Of course, having Miss Orpheo in the piano wasn't the same thing as having your own talent, but it was better than nothing. Especially when your parents made you go to a music school where nobody would talk to you. Hilary ducked just in time to avoid getting somebody's elbow in her eye.

"Children. Children!" The crowd parted as well as it could. Madame St. George, looking like a turkey in her long ratty-looking black-lace dress and her heavy clunking necklaces, strutted toward the auditorium. Behind her, bumping through the crowd, trailed Miss Edgeworth, squeezed into a tight fire-engine-red dress. Miss Edgeworth carried a notebook and a pencil and tried to look important. Holding her hands artistically, Madame St. George clapped twice, waved toward the auditorium, and with a grand flourish flung open the doors, as if to say, only *she* could do it. Then wheeling around dramatically, she announced, "*My* children, only. Please follow me." Miss Edgeworth scribbled something in her notebook. Hilary bet it wasn't anything.

A shiver of excitement ran through the lobby as the young performers picked themselves out of the crowd and followed Madame St. George into the hushed gloom of the empty auditorium. They trooped down the long center aisle where they spread out left and right to their seats in the first row. A second row of seats, immediately behind the children, had been reserved for trustees of the school and special friends of Madame St. George. Madame St. George always sat in the first seat at the extreme left, near the steps leading up to the stage. In this way, she could rise comfortably and announce each performer (as if the audience couldn't read the printed program).

Opening the auditorium relieved some of the congestion in the packed reception hall, and a stream of grateful people, properly subdued and respectful, began to flow into the seats of the recital hall. Pretty soon it was noisy again.

It was funny, Hilary thought, staring back at the people filling the seats behind her, but there was even a ritual for dressing for this kind of thing. The children, polished and starched, wore their best party clothing. The boys looked particularly unhappy in ties and jackets. But it was the little kids who were really sickening: puffed out like dolls in billowy dresses, ribbons in their hair, white socks. . . . Hilary noticed a very little girl in a dress covered with pink frills. Her blond curls were caught up on the top of her head and secured with a long pink ribbon. She looked like a valentine. Yich! Madame St. George was all dressed up in a long gown, dripping with jewelry. Her heavy earrings swayed like wattles from her ears. She acted like the Queen of Something, welcoming her subjects to the school.

Pointing, here, there, with her finger, Madame St. George herded the children into their seats, indicating special seats near her for her pets. "How lovely you look, dear," she gushed at Lyra Lyons, whose seat was practically under her nose. "No, No! You are a big boy! You can't sit there," she snorted at a halfway human-looking boy, about Hilary's age. "That seat is for my little lamb, my Angela." She looked around and finally found Angela standing right beside her. "Ah, Angela, darling, *there* you are." Madame St. George clapped her hands with delight. "You are a vision. Sit here, *ma petite*," she trilled at the little girl, "right next to me." Lyra Lyons glared at the little girl, who glared back.

"Angela darling" turned out to be the undergrown china doll in ribbons and pink frills, Madame Tarsatini's star pupil. Hilary felt like throwing up. She looked sympathetically at the halfway-human boy. He was busy eating his fingers and talking to the girl who sat next to him. This year Adrian Scorn was missing. His parents had taken him to Europe to continue his studies. Madame St. George must have loved that!

The lot-drawing ceremony came next. "There are nineteen children," Madame St. George announced. "Ten children will perform, and then we shall have a little intermission . . ."

The children groaned.

". . . a little intermission," continued Madame St. George, sharply, "during which you may join your parents and guests for lemonade and tea sandwiches, which Miss Edgeworth has so kindly prepared for us."

Miss Edgeworth acknowledged the compliment with a smirk.

"You will now draw a slip of paper from the bowl in Miss Edgeworth's hands." Miss Edgeworth, looking very pleased with herself, held the fishbowl aloft. "On each slip," continued Madame St. George, "Miss Edgeworth has been kind enough to print a number."

The children sat, tense and silent, while Madame St. George launched into her "I-Have-No-Favorites, Every-one-Knows-How-Fair-I-Am" speech. The children weren't listening. They were staring, almost hypnotized, at the fishbowl, which Miss Edgeworth continued to hold in front of them. Smiling and nodding at Madame St. George, the school secretary seemed completely indifferent to their agony.

When Madame St. George had concluded her remarks, the excited children crowded around Miss Edgeworth, who, as usual, offered first choice to her favorites. There were gasps and groans as the children opened their bits of paper. Hilary's turn came. She reached into the bowl and discarded the first two pieces of paper that came between her fingers. She didn't even know what number to pray for. Not the last. Certainly not the first . . .

She withdrew her hand from the bowl and, trembling, unfolded the little slip of paper. Number eleven. She gulped. That meant she would be the first to play after Intermission. It could have been worse. There was a shriek from the poor child who had drawn number one. The children had gotten very noisy. Letting off some of the tension that had accumulated during the lot-drawing ceremony, they kept hopping out of their seats, running back and forth comparing numbers and trying to swap.

Madame St. George held up her hand and called for silence. When everyone was settled, she drew herself up to her full height and, facing the nervous children, began her "Don't Hurry—Don't Worry (Don't Fall on Your Face)" pep talk.

"When your name is called, you will rise calmly . . ."

Led by the halfway-human boy, some of the children started to giggle. Madame St. George glared at the boy. Instantly there was silence. ". . . you will rise calmly," she repeated, "and go to the left side of the stage. There you will mount the steps" (the children groaned) "and proceed to the piano. Be seated."

Hilary's heart began to thump. She looked up at the enormous piano. Surrounded by an expanse of empty stage, the regal instrument stood proud and aloof, waiting impatiently. Even from her seat immediately below in the first row, the piano seemed thousands of miles away in another world. Hilary stared at the gleaming black instrument. The piano seemed to relax and soften. It grew friendlier—as if it knew Miss Orpheo was there. Hilary clasped her hands, concentrated, and prayed: "Please, please, Miss Orpheo, let it be good." Then, swallowing hard, she added, ". . . and *please*, no tricks!" For Miss Orpheo's benefit, Hilary silently reviewed the names of her pieces. It seemed crazy that a person could memorize all the notes of a piece, but couldn't remember *what* piece. One thing she wouldn't have to worry about, Hilary thought with a shiver, was the possibility of Miss Orpheo falling asleep. There would be enough noise to prevent that.

Madame St. George was still talking. "Once you are at the piano, take your time, children. Adjust the piano bench so that you are comfortable. We wouldn't want anyone to fall off, would we?" This was supposed to be funny. The children laughed uncomfortably.

Hilary glowered at Madame St. George. Why couldn't the stupid woman keep her mouth shut. It occurred to Hilary that it was Madame St. George, with her vanity and love of showing off, who made piano recitals such a competitive nightmare. If you could just get up quietly and play your pieces for a few people, without blowing everything into a Super Production, you wouldn't feel as if you were being eaten alive.

"Do not begin to play immediately," continued Madame St. George, sweeping up and down the front of the recital hall as she addressed them. She paused, wheeled about, and asked, "What will you do instead?"

"Put our hands in our laps and *think* about what we are going to play," they replied in straggly chorus.

"Very good," said Madame St. George. "And then what?"

"Put our hands on the keys and think again."

Hilary quailed. With all that putting and placing, you might get to the piano and find yourself STUCK. What a horrible thought! It was like letting yourself into an icy ocean inch by inch: you might never get in. It was much safer to gallop up on the stage, start your fingers moving in the air, and plunge in before you could think about it. Otherwise, you might suddenly see the audience, and if you didn't immediately have ten heart attacks, you might decide to fling yourself from the stage and run—while you still could.

Hilary glanced at her watch. It was five minutes to three. The recital hall was filling up. She squirmed around in her seat to see if her family had arrived. Not yet. She saw Miss Edgeworth, strutting like a chicken, hurrying to the front of the auditorium. She whispered something to Madame St. George.

Madame St. George frowned. She looked displeased. "Oh, really," she sniffed. Running her eyes along the row of children, she called out, "Hilary Banister! Is Hilary Banister here? There is a telephone call for you—in the office. Please hurry. I cannot hold an entire recital for one child."

Hilary's heart jumped. Feeling dizzy, she got up and pushed her way up the crowded aisle. Maybe something had happened to her parents? Remembering last year, maybe they had decided they couldn't bear to see her disgrace them? Maybe . . . maybe they were just late . . . or Waldo . . .

She grabbed the phone. "Hello?" She couldn't believe her ears. She shook the receiver.

"Hello, Hilary, is that you?" Miss Orpheo's voice came through the receiver. "May I inquire what number you are in the recital?"

May you inquire? Hilary felt herself go limp. "Eleven," she replied.

"Excellent. I shall be there in ample time," said Miss Orpheo.

"*Be there!*" screamed Hilary into the telephone. "Please, Miss Orpheo, this is no time for joking. Where *are* you?" she cried.

"I am not joking," said Miss Orpheo icily. "To the best of my knowledge, I am in B Altman and Company —a very pleasant store—fifth floor"—Miss Orpheo hesitated—"yes, northeast corner, to be precise. In a telephone booth. As for B Altman and Company, it is located on Thirty-fourth Street and . . ."

"Miss Orpheo, how *could* you?" cried Hilary in despair. She cupped her hand around her mouth so that no one would hear. "Don't you know what day it is? You're supposed to be . . ."

"Why, Hilary!" Miss Orpheo sounded shocked. "I never thought you would be so inconsiderate. Despite my lifelong devotion to music, I have absolutely no intention of risking life and limb beneath the hands of a bevy of juvenile performers. Perish forbid!" Miss Orpheo's voice changed, becoming confidential. "Quite frankly, Hilary, the Chopin 'Military Polonaise' is a dangerous piece. I noticed from the program that no less than three children intend to . . . er . . . play it. I am quite likely to be pounded insensible—if not worse," she added grimly.

Hilary shook the telephone receiver and her head to make sure she was hearing right.

"Dear me," continued Miss Orpheo. "The intolerable banging of the Lyons child, alone, is enough to decapitate a person. *You* are my pupil. I have undertaken to assist you. I shall do so. More than that you cannot ask."

Hilary felt sick. Miss Orpheo was quite mad. Drunk, maybe? She did sound a bit queer. Sort of giddy? No, Hilary decided, Miss Orpheo didn't drink. She wasn't the type. Maybe it was Hilary who was drunk—or dreaming? From the office, Hilary could see the front lobby. It was almost empty. Everyone was inside. She clutched the phone, squeezing it.

"What are you doing in Altman's?" she asked.

"Talking to you."

"Besides that?" screamed Hilary, raking her fingers through her hair. Her hair looked like a plow had gone through it.

"That is precisely why I called you. I have come to purchase a new frock . . ."

"You mean, a dress?"

"Yes, if you please. My work, you know, is very hard on clothing. Two dresses torn in the last six months."

"Why do you need a new dress, now?" Hilary screeched into the phone.

"Are *you* wearing a new dress?"

"Yes, my mother made me . . ."

"Well, then," said Miss Orpheo severely, "is there any reason why I, too, should not have a new dress? Although it is not exactly our debut, it *is* a public performance. I must say, the selection of dresses is not what it used to be. Neither are the prices!" she observed with a snort. "Nonetheless, I have found a perfectly lovely afternoon frock. As soon as I have made my purchase, I shall pop into the subway."

The SUBWAY! Hilary couldn't believe it. The woman was incredible. Outside, the lobby was completely empty. There was a burst of applause greeting Madame St. George as she rose to welcome her guests. The recital was about to begin. Oh God! Hilary groaned. Couldn't the old tightwad take a taxi?

"Please, Miss Orpheo, please hurry," Hilary begged. "I've got to go. They're beginning."

"Do go," said Miss Orpheo. "The only thing left for me to do, is to decide between the *blue* and the *brown*. Then I'll be . . ."

"Take the blue!" Hilary screamed into the phone. Ragpicker blue, ragpicker brown—what difference did it make?

But Miss Orpheo had hung up.

14

THE RECITAL

Hilary slid into her seat just in time. The recital hall was
hushed, the audience alert and tense. "And now," Madame St. George was saying, "we shall open our little recital . . . let me see . . ." She reached for her glasses,
which lay on her enormous bosom, suspended from her
neck by a gold chain—so they couldn't escape. "Ah,
yes," she said, squinting at the program, "Marcia Joy
Miller will play the Adagio from the 'Moonlight Sonata'
by Ludwig van Beethoven." (Madame St. George had a
way of giving a composer's first name as if there could
be another Beethoven—Jack Beethoven?)

The audience buzzed, coughed, shifted. Madame St.
George retired to her seat with a grand sweep, and Marcia Joy Miller, a tall, gawky girl with long arms shot
from her seat and dashed onto the stage as if pursued by

171

a ball of fire. Once safely seated at the piano, she plunged into the first movement of the "Moonlight Sonata," completely forgetting Madame St. George's instructions about waiting, and thinking, and taking your time. After a bumpy start, Marcia Joy settled down and the "Moonlight Sonata" flowed on, swelling, then gradually ebbing, in a slow glimmer of rippling tones. The last shimmering notes of the music died away and, grinning with relief, Marcia Joy bolted back to her seat to the enthusiastic applause of an audience not yet bored out of its mind. A soft, collective sigh ran across the front of the auditorium. Having pitied Marcia Joy for being first, the children envied her now for being *through*.

After that, a boy named Harold Mendelssohn played "Venetian Boat Song, No. 2," by Felix Mendelssohn, which made everybody titter. In his second piece, he had to play several sections with his hands crossed, so that he looked like he was hugging himself. Once, as he scissored his arms open and shut, crossing and uncrossing his hands, he reached high into the treble and almost fell off the seat. Finally, he untangled himself and, to everyone's relief, finished the piece.

A little singsong tune kept going through Hilary's head: *It could happen again. It would happen again.* If she messed up last year, why not this year too? "Please, oh please, Miss Orpheo," she prayed, "GET HERE!"

When Lyra Lyons was called, Madame St. George paused to say a few words. She stood next to Lyra, one hand resting on Lyra's head, as if she owned her, and announced that Lyra Lyons had been chosen to appear on a television program for talented young musicians.

Everyone gasped. Madame St. George said that the school was indeed honored. Lyra's parents, she said, should also be proud of their daughter. Then Lyra mounted the stage, bowed, seated herself, and with magnificent poise, waited for what seemed like a year until the audience was completely quiet. Slowly, she lifted her hands to the keyboard and waited again. Hilary admired her nerve. Then, at some inner signal, she pounced. Off and away she flew, ripping through a Scarlatti sonata like a flash of lightning. When Hilary tried to play that fast, all the notes crumpled together and mashed into a lump.

The Scarlatti was followed by an ear-splitting performance of Chopin's "Military Polonaise." Hilary grimaced. She could see Miss Orpheo's point about not wanting to be pounded to death. As she played, Lyra bent over the piano, giving the impression that in a burst of creative genius she was also composing the music.

The girl sitting next to Hilary got up and played a gooey piece by Grieg, mooning over the slow passages and swaying in her seat. Serena Lang (who had played first last year) tossed off a sonatina by a composer Hilary couldn't pronounce. She kept speeding up and slowing down, dramatically, if not musically. Hilary's stomach plunged and pitched. She felt like throwing up.

Arabella von Mess pranced across the stage. Hilary remembered: "Don't do the Mozart—the von Mess child is doing it!" Madame St. George was right. Arabella von Mess played the sonata very prettily. When Hilary played it, the music came out square and thumpy.

Up onto the stage, be seated, play, APPLAUSE, back to your seat . . . next child. Just like last year. The audience grew restless. People whispered. They gossiped, rattled newspapers, dozed, and from time to time, consulted their watches. It would be a long concert. One man worked a crossword puzzle. Several women used the time to write marketing lists. One lady was busy recopying an address book.

Hilary sat frozen in her seat, ticking off the performers. She was losing track. Each child brought her one step closer to . . . She didn't dare think of it. She was trembling. A series of shakes and shivers, radiating from some central source deep within her body, trilled down her arms to the tips of her fingers. Icy-cold and stiff, her fingers clutched one another for comfort and warmth. They were totally useless for playing the piano. It was exactly like last year, she groaned to herself. Clenching her teeth to keep them from chattering out of her mouth, Hilary decided the best thing to do was to sit on her hands. Maybe that would bring them back to life.

Pink Frills was mounting the stage, skipping out toward the piano, flipping ribbons and flounces as she went. A murmur passed through the audience. Pink Frills reminded Hilary of last year's Little Creep. Little Creep had gone to a professional music school. Hilary sighed. Pink Frills . . . Little Creep . . . it made no difference. There was one at each recital. Pink Frills was worse, though. She was probably ten, but she looked about four and a half. The audience loved it when you looked too little to play. The parents, and even the teachers, weren't interested in music. It wasn't a piano recital, Hilary decided. It was a nasty contest to see who had the smallest, cutest, loudest, fastest, best-playing child. Pink Frills was playing something splendidly noisy, spraying arpeggios, rolling off broken chords, and enjoying every moment of her time in the spotlight.

Poor Lyra Lyons! Pink Frills was a stab in the back. After a few swoopy passages, during which the music appeared to be making up its mind where to go next, it rounded a bend and caught the scent. Pressing hard, Pink Frills raced down the homestretch and slammed to a halt in an explosion of chords. The audience went wild and rewarded the little girl with waves of applause.

Hilary clutched her hands in agony. She tried to think of how the Bach went. *This is the way it goes—Up-Down, Up-Down* . . . She tried to fit her fingers to the theme. They were numb, frozen. She searched for the opening notes. Nothing came. NOTHING! She knew it! SHE KNEW IT! She was ready to scream. She was going to have amnesia . . . was *having* it, in fact. Quaking with fright, she tried to think of something simple: her own name. When she finally found the words—H i l a r y B a n i s t e r—she wondered who *that* was!

A boy who looked like a duck was slashing his way through the second "Military Polonaise" of the afternoon. Hilary slid down in her seat, twisting around to search the audience. Skimming across the faces in the rows behind, she found the Claxtons, and finally, in the row behind them, her parents with Aunt Ottilie and Uncle Archer. Waldo was there, next to her father, in a tie, with his hair combed! Cookie was next to him. She tried to catch Cookie's eye, but Cookie was staring into her lap playing with her eyeglasses. Uncle Archer and Hilary's father looked bored and out of place. Aunt Ottilie, dressed in a very fashionable fur-trimmed suit, was waving to someone. There was an empty seat next to her. Well, at least they didn't bring darling Sally Anne. Sally Anne was probably home preparing for her concert debut in Carnegie Hall! Aunt Ottilie hid her face behind her program and leaned past Uncle Archer to say something to Hilary's mother. Mrs. Banister whispered back. The ladies separated and stared straight ahead. Then their heads came together again. More whispering. Hilary ground her teeth. Why did they always have to talk? Couldn't they at least be polite?

But the person she was really looking for wasn't there. Frantically, Hilary scanned the door to the auditorium. Miss Orpheo wasn't back yet. If only she would get here! Hilary's freezing hands began to thaw out and sweat. She couldn't decide which was worse: to play with your fingers frozen solid, or slithering about in puddles of sweat. What a time to go shopping! Hilary moaned. She began to feel sorry for herself, then angry at Miss Orpheo . . . sorry . . . angry . . . SCARED. Maybe Miss Orpheo was waiting backstage. Damn! Where was she? What if she arrived too late?

A half-hearted flurry of applause interrupted Hilary's thoughts. The duck-faced boy had finished. The audience was getting impatient. Just in time, Madame St. George arose and announced that a brief intermission would follow, during which refreshments would be served.

With a happy bustle, the relieved audience got to its feet and slowly began to file out of the recital hall. Those children who had already played descended with delight on the lemonade and tea sandwiches. The others would have choked had they eaten anything.

"Hilareee! Over here, Hilary!" It was her mother calling. Hilary turned in the crowd and saw her parents trying to make their way over to her. Waldo, wiggling under people's arms, got there first. His plate was loaded with tea sandwiches.

"Is she in? Did you talk to her?" he whispered, his mouth clotted with chopped egg.

"Shh." Hilary was about to tell him what had happened, when her parents and Aunt Ottilie and Uncle Archer bore down on them.

"Well, dear, just a little more to go and we'll be hearing *you*," said her mother with a smile.

Before Hilary could answer, Aunt Ottilie said, "What a shame you didn't play in the first part. It's so awful to play after intermission." She took a sip of lemonade, made a face and sniffed "Hmmf. Sour! Fortunately," she continued, "Sally Anne never had to play at one of these *group* things. It's so barbaric, really!"

For once, Hilary agreed.

"I'm certain we'll all be very proud of Hilary this afternoon," said Mrs. Banister to her sister-in-law. "In the past two weeks, Hilary's hardly been away from the piano. Isn't that true, Hilary? You seem to have turned over a new leaf."

"You can say that again." Mr. Banister spoke up. "It even surprised me. To be quite frank," he laughed, "I'd kind of written you off for music." He rested his hand on her shoulder.

Hilary was dying—slowly, quickly, all at once.

People were chattering, laughing, and calling, "Here, HERE . . . over here." For some, the intermission was a celebration. For others, it just extended the agony. Uncle Archer pushed a glass of lemonade into Hilary's hand.

"Here, Hilary, old girl. A woman over there made me take it. Not quite my kind of drink, you know. You look pale . . . ha ha . . . have a swig of lemonade . . . ha ha . . . maybe it will help."

Hilary put up her hands in protest. She didn't want anything. Her mouth was so pasty, she couldn't even swallow. But Uncle Archer kept shoving the glass at her. Well, maybe, after all, the lemonade would help. She took the glass from her uncle, thanked him with a sick smile, and turned to Waldo.

"Where's Cookie?" she asked.

"Getting something to eat, I think. Where's Miss Orpheo?"

"Not here yet," Hilary snapped.

Waldo stared at her. "How come?"

"She went shopping." Hilary tried to make it sound sensible.

"Are you crazy? How could she . . ."

"Never mind."

"But . . ."

"I said, never mind! Forget it, Waldo. FORGET IT!" She didn't mean to yell at him, but it was just too much to explain.

Waldo shook his head slowly. Then he stuffed four sandwiches into his mouth. "Hey, Hil, try one of these blue ones. They're not bad." He offered it to her. But Hilary wasn't listening, so he ate it himself. Waldo adored anything that was free—even blue tea sandwiches.

The intermission was almost over. Hilary lifted the glass her uncle had given her and, with a shiver, took a long, deep drink, letting the thin lemonade wash over the thick fuzz coating her mouth. She took another swallow. How queer! There was something . . . Whhhaaaaat? She tilted the glass forward, held it in front of her, and stared into it. Her eyes converged at the bottom of the glass. She took another sip and held the glass away from her face, trying to see. It looked like letters . . . words . . .

OhmyGOD! Lemonade. Of course! There was something printed in the glass at the bottom of the drink. She swallowed some more lemonade and held the glass up to the light, squinting, trying to read the tiny words magnified in the thick glass at the bottom.

Loose wrists.
Count.

Hilary took another gulp of lemonade.

Watch pedal!

Another gulp. The lemonade receded still farther.

Play the Bach, Dear!

DO RE MI FA SOL—
Play the Bach.
    (signed) Miss Orpheo.

Hilary's eyes practically crossed as she tried to read the rest of the message. For the last time, she lifted the glass to her mouth, draining it completely. There was one more line.

P.S. I bought the brown—to match the Mazurka.
                    Yours faithfully,
                    P. Orpheo

"Well, it looks like intermission's over," boomed Uncle Archer, patting Hilary on the head, messing up her hair and practically knocking her unconscious. "Time to face the music, ha ha!" Hilary recoiled and ducked another pat. "Let's go." He gave Aunt Ottilie a swat on the rear. She glared at him.

Mrs. Banister said, "Oh, dear, I'm getting nervous myself. It's Hilary's turn next."

Mr. Banister said, "Come, let's get back to our seats and get it over with."

Waldo said, "Good-bye, Good Hope, Good Luck"— and squeezed his sister's hand.

Time was running out. Hilary sat in her seat, waiting in a state of controlled terror, unable to believe it was really happening to her. Oh, but it was. *Things* happened to *her*, she thought, recalling last year. Her breath came sharp and fast, sometimes not all. Waves of gooseflesh swept up her arms. She tried to calm herself by playing a grim little game. She would imagine The Worst:

O.K., she would forget everything. Miss Orpheo would play the wrong music, or fall asleep. O.K. People would break into wild laughter. She would be expelled from the school. (What was so bad about that?) Anything else? Hilary let her thoughts roam, searching, but nothing turned up. Now she forced her mind to return to the image of herself sitting at the piano while the audience sat there laughing. Horrible! She flinched and the image disappeared. Summoning courage, she made it come back again.

And then, suddenly, having taken a good, hard look at The Worst, she felt less frightened.

The audience had settled down—more or less. For those who had already played, the second half of the recital was a waste of time. Madame St. George arose to welcome her guests back. She stuck her glasses on her nose, tapped her hearing aid, and consulted her program. When she spoke again, Hilary thought she detected a certain sharp edge in her voice. It could have been Hilary's imagination, but the voice seemed to say, "Alas, every sunny day must have its cloud. Not everyone is imbued with the Spirit of Music, as . . . er . . . we discovered at last year's recital. Nevertheless, the Henrietta St. George Music School does not shirk its duty. We are always ready to lend a helping hand—even to musical cripples."

"Next on our program," Madame St. George was saying, "Hilary Banister" (yes, the voice *was* different) "will play the Mazurka in C minor, opus 31, by Frederic" (who else?) "Chopin, followed by the very lovely Invention in B-flat by Johann Sebastian Bach."

Hilary felt the challenge of "very lovely." Very lovely until played by Hilary Banister, is what Madame St. George meant. It was as if the old dragon wanted to disclaim responsibility for what was about to happen.

Her jaw stiff, her eyes glazed, Hilary sat staring straight ahead. Madame St. George, she noticed, had a bald spot on the top of her head.

"Hilary Banister!" Madame St. George announced.

"Hey, isn't that you?" Somebody gave her a poke. "It's *your* turn."

With a start, Hilary snapped out of her trance. Suddenly it hit her. *She* was the Hilary Banister they were waiting for! She had been sitting there like someone in the grip of a scary movie, tense, hardly daring to breathe, waiting to see herself walk out on the stage.

Like an arrow released from its bow, Hilary catapulted from her seat, flew up onto the stage, and found herself sitting in front of the enormous piano. She had no idea how she got there. A rustle of shifting seats and shuffling programs came from below in the audience. People coughed. She didn't dare look out at the sea of faces. The piano waited, its black and white teeth gleaming. The audience waited. Madame St. George waited. Miss Orpheo waited.

Hilary drew a deep breath and began to play. To her surprise, she heard the plaintive opening measures of the Mazurka emerge from beneath her fingers. Thanks to Miss Orpheo, the delicate grace notes went easily. The

music flowed, winding and curving, a dance of the heart
—passionate and melancholy. After a while, Hilary realized she was holding her breath. She exhaled in little
racking sighs. Her entire body relaxed and immediately
she felt better.

By the time she reached the second page—only of
course, there was no music in front of her—Hilary's
stomach had stopped zipping up and down, and her
hands had almost stopped trembling. She even dared let
her fingers (and Miss Orpheo) carry on for a split second while she listened to herself play. The audience
grew quiet and attentive. The no-man's-land between
stage and audience seemed to shrink as the audience
drew closer, enveloping her in its attention.

As on the night of her dream, she was filled with a
sense of uplifting joy and of great power. And a feeling,
not exactly of love, but certainly of gratitude to Chopin
who had provided the music. So this is what it was like
to be talented, to be a concert performer, she thought.
This is why they *wanted* to play! And with an eerie
sense of insight, she understood that as you played the
piano, you played *them*. She remembered the haunting
music she had heard that afternoon in the school library.
Armed with the magic of great music, you could *do*
something to them; and you could *give* them something
—something they might not even know they needed.
You could bend a rude, bored audience to your will; you
could command people's attention and respect. You could
make them love or laugh; you could bring tears to their
eyes or fill them with joy.

A long downhill diminuendo brought the Mazurka to

a close. There was a rewarding burst of applause, especially strong and lingering, it seemed to Hilary, in the center left of the recital hall where her family sat. Instead of the usual spray of polite handclapping, this was real applause, concentrated and aimed: the solid, rhythmic response of people who had been summoned from various distractions to listen to her and who liked what they had heard. Hilary smiled into the piano and thanked Miss Orpheo.

The applause subsided. Hilary lifted her hands and began the second piece. *This is the way it goes . . . Up-Down, Up-Down . . . This is the way it goes . . .* The two voices of the Bach Invention chattered back and forth, joyously answering and echoing each other. The piano bench, as usual, was a little too far out for comfort. No matter, she told herself almost gaily. Miss Orpheo would attend to things. She tucked her left foot around the bench leg, lifted herself slightly, and managed to wriggle the bench a little closer. There—that was better. The second theme entered, high-spirited and bouncy. Shaped and phrased by Miss Orpheo, the Invention sparkled and danced like water splashing in the sunlight. It sounded even better, Hilary thought, than on the night of her parents' party.

She couldn't see Madame St. George, who sat below and behind her, but Hilary could almost hear the little gasps of disbelief and shock as Madame St. George discovered that she had been all wrong about Hilary Banister. She wondered if Madame St. George might not even be a little disappointed at her pupil's failure to be predictably awful. Sweet victory!

Then a shadow fell. When you came down to it, of course, Hilary realized sadly, Madame St. George was right. It was really Miss Orpheo, knocking herself out inside the piano, they admired: Chopin, Bach, and Miss Orpheo. The person outside on the piano bench was still Hilary Banister, musical moron.

Hey! That was close. She almost missed a note. Pay attention! Hilary concentrated on the music, tensing slightly as she approached the Horrible Spot. Was there that much good luck in the world? Yes. She emerged from the difficult stretch, smiling. Now that it was safely behind, she played on, interweaving the two voices with a verve and dash she would never have risked without Miss Orpheo's assistance. And yet, she had to admit, practicing hadn't hurt. In fact, it had helped. For the first time, she had the feeling that she really had the music in her fingers. It had become part of her. She had worked so hard to keep her part of the bargain with Miss Orpheo that by now the music was permanently stamped in her brain. Confident, exhilarated by success, almost enjoying herself, Hilary entered the concluding passage. Her fingers flew along, interlacing the two voices of the Invention. The worst was over. In a few seconds she would be home safe.

Trusting her fingers and Miss Orpheo to finish their work, she actually dared to turn and steal a quick glance at the audience. This time she found them immediately. A magnet seemed to draw her through the vast blur of upturned faces. First, the Claxtons, and behind them, Cookie chewing her hair, listening intently; Waldo leaning forward, his chin resting on the seat in front; her fa-

ther and mother, smiling proudly; Uncle Archer, awake
for once; Aunt Ottilie, looking stunned. Hilary's eyes ran
across the long row . . . And then she almost stopped
playing.

There, in what had been the empty seat next to Aunt
Ottilie, engrossed in the music, sat Miss Orpheo in a
new brown ragpicker dress. With a gasp, Hilary jolted
back to the piano. Blindly, numbly, drifting in shock,
she let her fingers bring the music to a close. A volley of
applause burst from the audience. When Hilary turned
to look at Miss Orpheo again, the seat next to Aunt
Ottilie was empty.

Miss Orpheo was gone.

15

Afterward

One week after the piano recital, an advertisement appeared in *The New York Times* and the *American Music Teacher*. It read:

WANTED
Experienced Piano Teacher
Must Like Children
Excellent Salary

Applicants for the position were advised to present their credentials to Miss F. Edgeworth at the Henrietta St. George Music School. The address and telephone number were given.

After her remarkable success at the recital, Hilary continued her musical studies with Mr. André, who did not make her do the Loosening-up Exercises. She practiced hard and got along well with her new teacher. At the end of the school year, however, Hilary asked her mother if she could stop piano lessons. She couldn't see what use the piano would ever be to her, really. And anyway, she was on the tennis team for next year. In the seventh grade, she explained, they were going to have much more homework. She wouldn't have enough time to practice.

Mrs. Banister sighed and said it was a shame, just when Hilary was doing so well. She didn't approve of Hilary's giving up the piano, but—to Hilary's surprise—after thinking it over for a while, Mrs. Banister admitted that *this time* there were certain other factors to be considered. Mr. Banister had finally decided to remodel their apartment. It would be a huge job. The plans called for enlarging the living room by tearing down the wall between that room and the small inside hall. Mrs. Banister shuddered at the thought of the mess. For months the place would be a shambles of plaster and paint. But in the long run, it would be worth it. The new apartment would bear brilliant testimony to Simon Banister's genius.

At first Hilary couldn't believe they'd done it: she was finally free of piano lessons. And yet now that it had happened, she had an empty, disappointed feeling—almost as if she had needed them to say no, and instead they'd let her down.

The remodeling plans also called for new furniture, which Mr. Banister intended to design himself. The cumbersome grand piano would be sold and replaced by a small ultra-modern instrument designed and built by a friend of the Claxtons. The new piano was fantastic, according to Mrs. Banister, who had seen it. It was made of clear Plexiglas. It had no legs and was suspended with its attached bench from the ceiling by chains. The whole effect was marvelously airy, as if the piano and its bench were floating in space. Nobody in the family, said Mr. Banister, played well enough to require a piano as big as the old Steinway, which destroyed the "spatial flow" of the room. After all, one had to be realistic, Mrs. Banister apologized uncomfortably, the day the movers came to take away Mr. Ferdinand's beloved piano.

Waldo never took piano lessons. One day he announced that in music class he had been assigned the French horn. He was going to learn to play in school, and then he could be in the school band and get excused from Health Studies. Nobody was certain what a French horn was, until Mr. Banister suggested they look it up in the encyclopedia. According to the picture, the French horn was an impressive instrument—almost as big as Waldo. The idea seemed sensible. Waldo would have his lessons in school and could practice there, too, since it was impractical to lug such an awkward instrument home each day. Mrs. Banister thought it rather original to have a French horn player in the family. "It's different," she told Aunt Ottilie, who said the French horn was not a very feminine instrument, which is why Sally Anne had never played it.

Hilary never saw Miss Orpheo again. But once, in the National Museum in the city of Budapest in Hungary, a group of tourists were standing in front of a rare Broadwood piano that had belonged to Beethoven. They were staring at the piano awed by the thought that Beethoven's fingers had actually touched this instrument, when suddenly they were startled to see the keys begin to move. A brief passage of music (from the "Moonlight Sonata," according to one of the tourists) issued from the long-silent instrument. No one was near the piano, the bewildered tourists insisted, and they had *all* heard it play.

Another time, in the Chopin museum on the island of Majorca, off the coast of Spain, the night watchman reported that Chopin's piano had suddenly started playing *by itself*—and then, just as abruptly, had stopped. No one was in sight at the time. The watchman was fired for drinking.

One evening Mr. Banister was sitting in the handsome new living room reading his newspaper. "Well, how do you like that!" he exclaimed, looking up from his paper.

"Like what?" asked Hilary.

"Like what? What are you talking about?" cried Waldo, jumping up and down impatiently when there was no answer.

"Yes, dear, do speak up," said Mrs. Banister.

"It's an incredible story," said Mr. Banister. "It seems that a very valuable grand piano in a Steinway showroom suddenly started playing ALL BY ITSELF!"

Waldo raised his eyebrows and glanced at Hilary.

"That's impossible," said Mrs. Banister. "There must be some reasonable explanation."

"Noooo . . ." said Mr. Banister, reading and shaking his head. "No . . . there isn't. It's probably a hoax."

"Let me see that please, Dad!" cried Hilary, swooping across the room and snatching the paper from her startled father.

"Well, of all the . . . What's come over *her?*" exclaimed Mr. Banister, staring at his empty hands.

"It's one of those days. Growing pains I guess," said Mrs. Banister, shaking her head. "It's a hard age. Everyone says so. And it gets worse . . ." she added darkly.

In her room, Hilary closed the door, opened the paper, and began to read. The headline said: "HAUNTED PIANOS—STILL NO EXPLANATION." According to the newspaper article, the most recent incident in the mysterious outbreak of pianos that played by themselves had occurred in a showroom of Steinway and Sons in New York City. A salesman was showing a beautiful concert instrument to a customer, a well-known pianist, when suddenly the piano began to play. It played a few measures of a Chopin Mazurka, followed by the opening line of Bach's Two-Part Invention in B-flat. Then it stopped. The newspaper printed the music the piano had played.

Hilary stared hard at the familiar music and read the article again. A long tremor, like open space, streaked through her fiber, leaving a mark that, though it came and went, would never entirely leave her as long as she lived. She shook herself, folded the paper carefully, and gave it back to her father.

That was all.

JUDITH GROCH is a native New Yorker who attended Vassar College and graduated from Columbia University, where she was elected to Phi Beta Kappa. She has written humor and fiction for a number of magazines and is the author of the book *You and Your Brain*, which won the 1963 Thomas Alva Edison Foundation Mass Media Award for the best science book for youth. She has also written an adult book, *The Right to Create*. Judith Groch works as an editor for a medical newsmagazine. PLAY THE BACH, DEAR! was inspired by the experiences of her children who have all studied piano. And, of course, she takes piano lessons, too.